Lurking Miscellany

A collection of short fiction

D.A Lascelles

Lurking Miscellany

A catalogue record for this book is available from the British Library.
ISBN 978-1-907308-89-5

Published by Compass Publishing

For more copies of this book, please email:
dalascelles-writing@yahoo.co.uk

Cover Designed by Skyla Dawn Cameron
http://indigochickdesigns.blogspot.co.uk/

Printed in Great Britain

Acknowledgements

With thanks to Sarah Lascelles, Ed Fortune, Dave Hawkins, Maria Frank, Chris Shepherd, Chris Snook and Dom Parry for their contributions to the worlds portrayed in here and a great deal of kudos to Russ (R.A) Smith, Thomas Spychalski, Ninfa Hayes and Judy Bagshaw for beta reading. Thanks are also due to Nick Alhelm (of Metahuman Press) for his advice, Erica Hayes for daring me to write out of my comfort zone and Macallister Stone and the other contributors to the Absolute Write forums for a lot of random stuff. Finally, thanks to all the Waypoint LRP players and crew, especially Emily Wilcox for being Orchil and Dave Lowry for Lt. Icarus.

Foreword

I called this collection Lurking Miscellany for two reasons. One was as a not too subtle reference to my blog, Lurking Musings. I've appended the word 'Lurking' to a few things, starting with my first Live Journal personal blog and ending with my more professional writing blog and it seemed appropriate. The word miscellany refers to the nature of the collection. It is a random collection of 'things found in the gutter of my hard drive' – old short stories that I wrote, maybe tried to get published, but largely just left in my hard drive gathering dust in the vague hope that I might one day develop the ideas further.

Some of these ideas were started as ideas for novels. One is the sequel to an existing novella. I think that they all have potential to be taken further. With that in mind I would like those who read this collection to voice an opinion on which of these they liked the best. There will be ways for you to do this listed at the end of this book.

Page 7 - An Element of Desire

Sometime in the mid 90's I had an idea for a British sort of a superhero character who was ecologically minded and could control the elements. A friend from university had the idea for a time travelling psychic sports reporter. One night we decided to try to merge them into one story. It never worked out because we could never find the time, but I was left with a character in need of a story. This idea came to me after a trip to the now long demolished Jilly's Rockworld in Manchester. It is still sort of a part of that novel, an aside occurring in-between chapters, so there is room for more to be written in the future.

Page 32 - Dances with Drums

The Waypoint universe is one I have a lot of fondness for – a vast galaxy of different races who were once part of a huge empire but are separated by the now very unreliable hyperspatial gate network. It was created for a science fiction live action roleplay game I ran right up until 2008 when the final game brought large battles, alien invasions and the characters enacting a major change in the setting. Then, there was a call for submissions for an anthology with a music theme and I decided to develop an idea from the setting that involved drums and one of my favourite Dagdan shaman.

Page 61 - Triptych of the Gates

This is another Waypoint story, this time an attempt at a flash fiction which sort of failed by being too long for flash. Technically it is three flash fiction pieces linked by a common theme, hence the triptych of the title - three snapshots of the lives of three very different GateTechs.

When this story was critiqued, several said that they wanted to read more of it so I began to develop it as a novel. The extracts here were recordings of the thoughts and feelings of the characters made by a technology linked to the hyperspatial gate network. They became intros to sections where these characters played a part. I am still working on this novel and hope one day to finish it.

Page 78 - Transformations

This story came about because of a call for submissions involving concepts of transexualism. So I started with the concept of a character who was the ultimate in gender fluidity and then realised that I needed ordinary characters to contrast with that. Not one to reinvent the wheel, I used the characters I had created for Transitions, my paranormal romance novella. I even managed to get the title to fit with the theme, making this a true sequel.

Of course, I do not need any excuse to use Helen in a story. She is by far my favourite character.

An Element of Desire

"Oh my god! What is he doing?"

Simon heard Liz's cry at almost the same time as he saw the flashing light on the device on the side of the ship. It was an ugly bundle, wrapped in shiny black tape and wired to a crude electrical timer. He could feel the potential in it, an explosive force that was about to be released.

What the hell happened to the concept of peaceful protest, he thought as he jumped down from where he had been scrawling his slogan on the side of the oil tanker. He rushed to where the bomb had been planted. He knew he did not have much time, seconds maybe, but he also knew that he didn't actually have to get to it. He just had to put himself between it and the other protesters.

He raced across the dock, through the pools of light created by the security lamps designed to keep people like him out and came to the foot of the ladder where that stupid bastard Nightarse, or whatever the hell he called himself, was climbing down having planted the bomb.

"What the fuck do you think you are doing?" he shouted up at him.

"Saving our movement, what d'ye think I'm fucking doing?" He jumped off the ladder, looking smug as always. Simon had never liked the bastard; his arrogant self assurance annoyed the hell out of him and now he had gone too far.

Simon felt a hand on his shoulder.

"We have to get out of here," Liz said with urgency. "That thing..."

He shook his head. "Too late," The whisperings of the elements, the voices he always heard in his mind as they communicated with him, had already told him all he needed to know about this situation. "The fucker set the timer wrong, it's going to..."

He felt Fire's exhalation of pleasure a nanosecond before the flame blossomed out of the bomb and enveloped them all. He closed his eyes and held his arms out wide, hoping like hell he had enough control over Fire's impulsive destructive nature to pull this off. *You don't want me to die, do you?*

The flames surrounded him and Liz but did not touch them, and the shrapnel that flew from the wreckage was caught in mid-air and flung aside. Through the fire he saw the idiot who called himself Nighthawk, out of some pretentious posturing, caught in the blast that he had created, his body burnt and broken and flying to the ground. Part of him, a dark and secret part, was glad the idiot died after being so stupid but the rest of him hated that part for being so callous.

As the flames died, leaving the dockside in scorched darkness once again, Simon was thankful that he'd at least managed to save Liz.

***

"Look, don't fret it mate." Russell's voice shocked Simon out of his reverie as he approached the table with a couple of full glasses. "Ye'll work yourself into a depression and then no girl will ever want you again." He put the drinks down and shuffled into the alcove.

"Can't help it. Maybe I shouldn't have come out tonight. I've only made everyone feel down." He looked around the alcove. Apart from Russell it was empty. Not long ago it had been lively with friends. All of them had made excuses and left early.

Russell waved his hand dismissively. "Meh, you needed to get out of that house. Look, she dumped you and that's all there is to it. Either win her back somehow or move on."

"She dumped me for a damned good reason."

It was past midnight and the club was winding down. The frenzied dancing of the previous few hours had passed and slower, more sensuous tracks were playing. Couples were on the dance floor, swaying in each others' arms as the smoke and lights danced around them. Single people lurked on the outskirts, in dark alcoves, their shadowed faces watching the dance-floor eagerly, hoping that someone might pick them for slow dancing.

Simon, dressed in a tattered denim waistcoat and faded black T-shirt, knew only too well how they felt. As he leaned back in his alcove, his glass held tightly in his hand, he was also fixing his eyes on the dancers and remembering a time when he had been one of the envied. Back when Liz still thought of him as a human being and not some weird freak of nature.

He shuddered as he remembered the bowel trembling, cold sweat soaked moment when he'd seen the bomb on the side of the oil tanker and realised that some moron was trying to turn their peaceful protest, nothing more than some environmentally aware graffiti, into a terrorist attack. He'd told everyone that Liz had left him because of this. That she had been horrified by the extremes some environmental activists went to. The truth was that he had called it off, too scared of the potential risk to her. She had watched as he'd caused the explosion to warp around them and had been full of questions about what had happened which he did not feel up to facing. The argument had stemmed from his sullen silence in response to all her questions.

Russell shrugged. "Well, there are worse reasons to be dumped. Look, how about you come to this protest tomorrow. I promise no bombs. Just leaflets."

"Maybe," Simon brushed a strand of his dirty blond hair out of his eyes, took a deep drink of his pint and grinned at his companion. "Yeah, why not. It'll cheer me up."

"So, ye'll come along? That's great." Russell's face lit up in pleasure at the news. "We'll show 'em the truth, and you being there will just max it up."

"Yeah, I'll be there waving banners and giving out leaflets as usual." Simon sighed, bored by the monotony of the concept. The rumours of what had happened at the oil tanker protest had circulated far and wide in the environmentalist community. There'd been frenzied discussions about it on web forums and conspiracy theories abounded.

Luckily, no one had yet mentioned anything supernatural and neither Liz nor any of the other participants had confirmed or denied any rumours but Simon was slowly being seen as something of an activist superhero. He hated that with a passion.

"Cool. Nine a.m., City centre. Corner of Driscoll Street. I'll see you there." Russell emptied his drink and stood up. "Look, mate, I have to go. Things to organise, you know how it is. You coming?" Simon shook his head. "No, no. I'm not ready to go yet." He picked up his glass to show that it was still almost half full. He'd been sipping where Russell had been gulping. He took another sip now and settled deeper into the alcove. Russell sat back down, a concerned look on his face.

"Are you sure you're OK? Do ye want to talk about it?"

Simon shook his head. "I'm fine. Don't worry about me." *I just want to be left alone.*

Russell paused for a moment, clearly carefully weighing up what he had to do against the importance of a friend in need. Finally, he sighed. "Ok, fine. You stay here and get drunk and feel sorry for yourself. I'll see you tomorrow. Call me if you decide you want to talk about it."

He stood up and walked away through the throng of the night club. Simon watched him go, sipping at the remains of his own drink. He was far from alone, however. As always his thoughts were filled with the voices of the Spirits.

Too peaceful, too placid. Why not do it like we did last time; burn and flame? Fire's insistent voice burnt at his mind, its litany of destruction flickering endlessly. *Leaflets and protest are no good, no one will ever pay attention to that!*

Simon did not answer Instead, Earth's ponderous tones lumbered into his mind. *No sense in being hasty; you cannot build any future on unsound foundations. No sense in destruction if there is nothing to replace it, no rebirth waiting to occur.*

There are benefits in being slow and careful. This was Water, tinkling gently. *One particle at a time, carried away into the stream forever.*

It was an old argument that the spirits had been having for as long as he could remember. He was not surprised by any of it, nor by the fact that Air seemed to be staying quiet. The spirit of Air rarely kept its attention on one thing long enough to form any sort of opinion. He could sense it, dancing among the spotlights of the club, playing chaotic games with the particles from the smoke machine.

Simon often wondered why he, of all humans in the world, had ended up with the ability to sense, communicate with and occasionally summon into being the elemental spirits. It was just something he had always been able to do and he remembered those awkward, early days at school when he'd innocently talked about it to others in his class and been surprised when no one else knew what he was talking about. He'd soon learnt to keep quiet.

He looked around the club, taking in the shabby decor and languorous patrons. With Russell gone there was no one left for him to talk to and he was in no mood for lone drinking or dancing. It was time to make a move. He had an early start in the morning if he was going to make that protest.

He stood up and made his way across the dance floor, weaving between the remaining dancers. Here and there in the boiling mass he could make out a pattern that was not natural, a place where Air had flitted in and scattered the dust. He could feel the other elements as well. Water: he could see in the flow of sweat from the brows of the dancers and in the plumbing that ran through the club like a metallic vascular system. Earth: he could feel in the throbbing of the music beneath his feet. Even Fire was there, though in a dormant state; in the fuel that filled lighters and in the potential that everything had to burn. It was sometimes distracting to be so aware of these sensations all the time, not to mention hearing their voices in his head. It took a lot of his focus to keep his mind on the world around him and sometimes, when he allowed his attention to slip, it caused problems.

Like now.

"Oooof!" The young woman he had bumped into stumbled and he reached out to catch her before she fell. There was a squeaky crinkling sound as his arms wrapped around her waist and as he pulled her up to her feet, his fingers slipped over the smooth blackness of PVC. He noted her smell next. It was thick and cloying, a hint of cigarettes smoked out in the rain, a touch of some perfume he could not quite identify and... something else... Something that tugged at his emotions, made Fire scream in his heart to take her in his arms and make her his.

He unwrapped his hands from around her back and stepped back, shocked by the intensity of his reaction to her.

"Sorry, so very sorry. Um, are you ok?"

She smiled up at him. "Sure, I'm fine. Should just learn to look where I'm going." Her smile reached deep into his libido and pulled a number of random levers, sending hormones rushing.

Her face was smooth and round and framed with long, dark hair that drifted lazily about her like smoke. Black painted lips and eyes contrasted sharply with her pale face. The effect of the make-up, the black hair and the shiny black PVC dress she was wearing was a collage of striking contrasts, a 1920's photograph. For a brief second, Simon believed that she had come from a different world, one where the only colours were black and white.

"Me too." He grinned at her. "Er, I'm Simon. Can I, uh, buy you a drink to apologise?"

She bit her lower lip and several more of those levers in Simon's libido were pulled. Her dark rimmed eyes looked up at him with an 'I know what you are up to' cast to them.

Let me have her! She is mine, I must have her! Fire's insistent call flared on in his mind, but he ignored it.

"Yeah, sure. Buy me a drink, why not?" Her voice was a silken whisper. She led the way to the bar, letting him see her from the back in a way which meant he could not fail to notice the shape of her body beneath the PVC. Her movements were so smooth it was as if she slithered across the floor rather than walked. With a smile on his face, he followed her, taking out his wallet as he approached the bar.

***

Back in the secluded booth that Simon and Russell had shared not all that long ago, she immediately made her intentions clear to him by squeezing up as close as she could despite there being plenty of space. The nature of this encounter was so very different to the quiet conversation about the environment he had been having earlier that Simon was having trouble reconciling both as being part of the same night. With her there, pressing close to him, it was hard to believe that there was anything else in the world.

"So, what do you do?" She sucked on one of the straws that protruded from the complicated and expensive cocktail he'd bought for her, looking straight at him over the forest of stirrers and foil decorations.

"Oh, nothing interesting." He tried to look casual as he took a gulp of his own drink, but his shaking hands betrayed him and sloshed beer all over the table between them. "Boring office job. You? You haven't told me your name yet, by the way."

"No, I haven't." She smiled a secret smile. "I'm a chemist, just got back from doing some great work over in Louisiana."

"America? Wow, must have been great. Wait, wasn't that where that oil spill happened? Were you there during that?"

"Yeah, the beaches were covered in it. I spent a lot of time there."

Simon nodded in understanding. Clearly this was a woman with a social conscience, spending her spare time helping to clear up oil spills on foreign beaches. It was exactly what he would have done, had he been near enough to do so. The day that spill happened, he'd woken up feeling sick, with Water raging and frothing at him about the poison afflicting it. He still felt the effects□□ a dull ache in his gut, weeks after the spill.

"So, you are, er, into the environment, then?"

She flashed a more open smile. "Oh yeah," she purred. "I am all over the environment. It can't get enough of me."

"That's great, really great. You could□um, come with me tomorrow to the protest?"

"The protest?"

"Yeah, it's in the City Centre. Raising awareness, posters, leaflets, charity collection, that sort of thing."

Stupid arse, that's a great pick up line. Hey, babe, why not come and stand in the street in the rain first thing in the morning, shouting at people about dead seagulls.

"Hmm, well, I am sure we can decide what we want to do tomorrow morning. After we wake up..." Her smile this time was cheeky and her eyes sparkled in the flashing lights of the club.

Wow. So blatant. This woman is amazing. Simon found himself aroused by her forwardness.

He raised his eyebrow at her. "I reckon we can do that."

Be careful, you know nothing about her... Earth was, as ever, over cautious. Steady, solid, rumbling disapproval.

She smells wrong. Air flitted past to make one of its rare contributions. Always changeable, was Air, the direction of its opinion varied greatly and it was rarely consistent. However, on occasion it was possible to see a pattern in the chaos.

I want her. Fire was hungry. Fire was always hungry.

Water was mysteriously silent. The depths of its silence radiated disapproval at the volume of a raging storm.

Simon blanked out the incessant spirit voices and took a long drag on his drink, building up his courage. "Let's go."

***

They started kissing as they made their way out of the club; a frantic lip-locked stumble through dancers, drinkers and bouncers. As they emerged into the cool, night air they stopped for a while, pressed against the wall of the club while they explored each others' mouths with their tongues and their bodies with their hands. Simon found himself enjoying the feel of the PVC, warmed from her body heat, and the strange scents that wafted from her. Combined with the fierceness of her reciprocated desire for him, it was intoxicating.

And yet, there was still a niggling doubt hanging in the back of his mind.

"I still don't know your name," he said, breathless in a break between passionate kisses.

Never mind names, I burn for her. Let me burn for her!

She put her finger on his lips. "Isn't it better to have the mystery? I could be the mystery girl, the one you never see again."

He brushed a stray wisp of hair from her face, only one strand from the boiling mass that poured from her head and down her shoulder and back. "I want to know you more than that."

"Aw, that is so sweet." She kissed him again, rubbing herself provocatively against his body as she did so. "I wish they were all as sweet as you."

All? Simon frowned. Of course he was under no illusions that this girl had been saving herself only for him. He let it slide, however, as another round of kissing began. He realised that his hand was touching her breast and also that it felt a little strange but he could not work out why. It was softer than he would expect, almost fluid. For a brief moment he was convinced that he could feel his hand sinking into the slippery, liquid plastic of the dress; that a tar-like substance was sucking him in. He almost pulled back in surprise but to do so would have meant breaking the kiss. He did not want to do that. He kept his lips pressed to hers and ignored the feeling.

She pulled away. Her thick black lipstick smeared across her face. "Come on, let's get a taxi."

He looked confused. "A taxi?"

"Sure, you think I'm going to fuck you in an alley? Silly boy!"

She took his hand and led him off down the street.

***

They kissed all the way back to the small flat she called home. The inside of the taxi was rank with something that smelled like burning plastic and evaporated petrol. Simon had the urge to tell the taxi driver that his engine must be in need of tuning or there was a leak somewhere but he was too focussed on the woman to worry about it.

He held her from behind and kissed her bare, white neck as they left the taxi and made their way to her house. With the door unlocked, she turned to face him, putting her arms around his neck and dragging him in. As the door slammed shut behind him, she led him towards her bedroom, walking backward in her high heels.

He did not get anything like a proper look at the flat. His eyes were all for her. He got an impression of sleek modernity, lots of chrome and plastic and a lack of clutter. Despite that, something about the place made him uneasy, a slight oppressive feeling that nagged at his consciousness, but he was too involved to pay any attention. He kicked off his shoes and felt the smooth linoleum floor beneath his feet, smooth enough to almost make him slip.

They entered the bedroom, still kissing, her still walking backwards. As the back of her knees touched the bed, she threw herself backwards to land spread-eagled on top of the duvet, her hair spreading darkly on the pale blue cover. She held up her arms and reached towards him as he stood at the end of the bed, beckoning him to join her.

He knelt on the edge of the bed, positioned his arms so that they supported him, and crawled towards her. As he fell into her arms, there was a creak from the bedsprings and a crackling squeak from her dress. As his hands brushed the duvet cover, he felt a static discharge. She pulled his face down towards her and kissed him fiercely.

"Oh, I am so going to enjoy this."

"Me too," he replied, grinning.

He put his hands down to where her dress met the bare flesh of her legs and began to work the dress up over her hips, kissing her all the time. She raised her eyebrows at this and began to undo the top button of his jeans

Something screamed in Simon's head then, splashing and raging against a cliff face of solid rock. He could not make out the words. One of the spirits was trying to tell him something, but it sounded muffled, as if smothered by a thick liquid. He ignored it, pushed it deeper down to allow him to focus more on what she was doing. By now she was pulling off his trousers, sensuously rubbing her hand over him. The mental noise persisted as the distant sound of surf, too distant to be sure if it were real or merely the illusion of the sea heard inside a shell. A viscous burbling, spattering as the sound tried to escape. Something was very wrong, and Water was trying to warn him.

He lifted his head, causing her to look up at him concerned.

"You okay, lover?"

He ignored her and looked down at his hands and her body. One hand, held behind her back, seemed to be trapped by her body. The other, reaching up the dress, was stuck in what felt like a thick liquid. As he'd risen up from her, droplets of the same black, sticky liquid had stuck to his chest and were now oozing from his body to reform with her dress anew.

"What the hell?"

She smiled at him, all pretence at concern gone. Her hair was flowing around her, oozing and staining the bedcovers.

"Such an old fashioned concept, Hell. The silly thing is people rarely work out that they are making their own Hell right here on Earth."

"But you... You're..."

"Sucking you right in, yeah." She giggled as his hand slipped another few inches, deeper into the black sludge that her entire body was made of. "You were easier to get than I'd anticipated. I had a whole host of seduction plans worked out for when you spurned me the first time. But here you are, all mine. I am so flattered you fell for me so easily, or are you really that desperate or stupid?" She giggled.

Incredibly desperate and stupid, he thought.

He struggled to pull his hand out, but that just caused it to sink in even deeper. She squirmed in pleasure.

"Ooh, do that again! I like that." She giggled as he struggled even harder and only succeeded in sinking even deeper until his arm was trapped up to his elbow.

"Now, not many men can honestly say they've gone *that* deep." She whispered into his ear as she wrapped her arms around him and pulled him back down into her chest. He started to sink, the black fluid rising up around him. Her head came up, her neck stretching to reach his face. He strained away as much

25

as he could in an attempt to escape; twisting and pulling, but aware that his struggles were only making things worse. Her lips reached for his. He wrenched his head to the side, escaping the hungry maw of her mouth which widened impossibly in its quest to engulf him.

"It's nothing personal, my lover." Her voice was sweet and apologetic. "It's just that you are a threat to my employer. Can't have you with your empathy for the planet and your contacts with the metaphysical elemental forces stopping our plans for the Earth now, can we?

"Better you're dead, anyway. That way you don't see what a mess we'll make of the place. I plan to cover the oceans, just as I am drowning you in me now."

Her lips came up, smeared black lipstick blending into once white flesh which was darkening to match. Her jaws opened, then widened. Stuck as he was, he could no longer move out of the way. They closed around him and he was trapped in darkness.

Despair hit him then. He couldn't breathe; the thick fluid covered his entire head, slowly crushing his chest. He was trapped. His open mouth was slowly filling with fluid. Her smell was everywhere, and now he realised what it was that he'd somehow been missing.

She'd beguiled him, turned his mind away from what it should have been noticing and thinking about, blocked him from his spiritual friends so they could not warn him easily and, when they did, put him in a position where he did not care about what they were saying.

Let me have her, let me take her. I want her! I want her so badly! Fire was screaming, more easily able to penetrate the blocks she had created because, Simon now realised, of its very nature. Water was smothered, as it always was by her kind. Air she could too easily poison. Earth, though stolid and dependable in most things, was hard-pressed to work against even a corrupted child of its own making. But Fire had a love for her that burned brighter than anything.

The smell had been the smell of long chain hydrocarbons, the long chains that made up the composition of crude oil. As his mind raced through these thoughts, Simon struggled against her, his lungs burning as he tried to struggle free from her choking grip. If his guess was right then she was some form of spiritual representation of oil, an aspect related to pollution. If that were the case...

His legs kicked involuntarily against the bed as the last of the oxygen in his lungs was lost to him. He concentrated and called upon Fire, unleashing it from the control he normally kept it under. He heard the crackling spurt of joy as the spirit leapt free and manifested around him. His own body, starting to sink into hers, caught light – flaring brightly with dancing, orange flames. She screamed.

The sticky oil burned away from his face and he could see her body melting onto the bed; spreading a thick, black, flaming ooze all over the sheets. Black smoke, reminiscent of her hair, billowed up from the fire, filling the small bedroom. Somewhere in the building a smoke alarm screeched. He rose from the flaming bed, untouched by the flames that he had called into being. All around him, other parts of the room were beginning to catch light as flames and sparks leapt from the bed. The carpet was already starting to smoulder under his feet.

The smoke made it difficult to navigate out of the bedroom and, as soon as he opened the door, it began to fill the other rooms as well. He coughed out a command to Air who whooshed to protect him from the toxins, blowing the smoke back away from him with a strong breeze. The door was ahead of him and he wrenched it open and staggered, still burning and coughing, out into the cool, early morning air. Other alarms started to wail and the sprinklers kicked into play as the fire system noticed the conflagration, spraying everything with a fine mist. Almost as an afterthought, Simon called on water and increased the pressure in the system. The pipes in the walls and the sprinkler system in the apartment exploded, splashing over the fire with a smoky hiss. He walked out through the door with the black smoke and steam around him like a halo.

Safe in the car park of the block of flats, he gently re-asserted his control over Fire. The flames around him died away, leaving him unmarked save for the blackening smut of the smoke that had stuck to his skin. This soot was all he had to remind him that she had even been there, a smearing corpse on his skin.

As the other residents of the tower block evacuated from the building and bustled around him, he heard the inevitable sound of sirens getting louder as they approached the building. Without thinking, he ran, dodging into a nearby side street and putting the building, the smoke and his encounter with the weird oil elemental as far behind him as he could.

He was breathless when he finally came to a stop, leaning against the chipped paint of the railings that surrounded a churchyard. Looking around, he could still see a plume of black smoke and the flashing lights of the fire engines a few streets away.

That thing, that... whatever the hell it was. He could not comprehend what he had just encountered.

He knew he had to run; as there would have been questions, and besides, one assassin had failed; what were the chances of another? That, whatever it was, the dark side of the honey trap, was obviously the first salvo in a crusade to wipe him out.

He pulled out his mobile and held it in his hand, looking down at it. He needed to talk to someone, someone he could trust. He also needed someone to keep him grounded. Russell was a good friend but not the most reliable person. The other people he knew were not close. There was really only one person he could turn to and she was the very person he did not want to get involved in all of this. He tapped his phone on the palm of his hand, working through the arguments, looking for a way to justify making that call.

No matter how he weighed the evidence, it all came out with him living a life alone and facing all this weirdness by himself.

He sighed and went to put his phone away, but then paused and pressed the button that lit up the screen. He scrolled through the contacts until he came to Liz's number. He paused, his finger hovering over the screen. Could he really do this? Could he really *not* do this was probably the question he should ask. It may not be safe for her to be part of this world, he reflected as he clicked, 'dial' and held the phone to his ear, but he realised that it had to be her choice whether she got involved with him or not. Besides, it was safer for him if she were around. Someone had to keep his feet on the ground and stop him from playing dangerous games with Oil elementals.

The phone clicked and a tired-sounding voice came out of the speaker. "Yes?"

He smiled at hearing her voice. "Liz, look, sorry to call so late. In fact, sorry for everything. I was an arse and I was, uh, wondering if I could come round. To talk."

He was relieved when her answer was a guarded, "Yes."

Dances with Drums

The sounds of drumming echoed through the trees as the black clad, helmeted squad emerged from the Gate. They took up defensive positions around the clearing, guns pointing down to show they were not an immediate threat but eyes scanning carefully for danger. Apart from the small delegation sent to meet them, a small group of warriors dressed in fur and leathers and leaning on spears at the edge of the clearing about 300 metres away, there were only the drummers – a small ring of around 10 of the crudely dressed aliens, known to other races as Dagdans, each one tirelessly beating out the same series of rhythms. A brief codeword from the Sergeant in charge through the subspace radio was enough to notify the base crew that all was well and allow the rest of the group through.

Specialist Investigator third class Doctor Caitlin Jowista was the next to step through the swirling energy pattern of the Gate. As she did so, she carefully lifted the visor of her helmet and looked down at the small, handheld device in her hands. The various graphs and digital readouts reassured her that all was well, their journey through Gatespace had been successful. Not only had they survived, and given the high fatality rate of gate travel that was no small feat, but they seemed to have ended up at the correct co-ordinates. To the soldiers she travelled with on a regular basis it did not seem such an achievement but Jowista knew better. She had read the plethora of articles in the Gatetech journals about the unreliability of the network. The chance of navigation error or death was alarmingly high.

She clipped the scanner to her belt, pulled the helmet off her head and turned to face Captain Johannus Lewis, Mission CO. "Right place and all present and correct, sir."

Lewis nodded to acknowledge her comment as he peeled off his jumpsuit to reveal the polished and pressed glory of his dress uniform – his rank tabs and the silver sheen of the Imperial star on his breast shining in the flickering gate energies. He signalled to Lieutenant Cross who brought over a long, thin box he had strapped to his back alongside the rucksack they all wore. He gently opened this and extracted an ornate, ceremonial sword. Holding it up in front of his face he carefully checked it for damage, examining the elegant filigree of the basket hilt and the smooth edge of the blade in the light of the sun. Satisfied, he attached it to his belt.

"Let's get this farce started then, shall we Doctor?"

The complex and overlapping rhythms of the drums danced in the ozone rich air as they marched into the clearing. It stalked them, seeming through some aural illusion to follow them through the woods. Jowista found the music fascinating, the rhythm was complex and she found herself obsessing over working out the sequence. She could never be certain where and how she would next encounter a note or a beat.

She wasn't sure she could decide which was worse, the ubiquitous drumbeats bouncing through the tall, the alien trees that surrounded them, or the paranoid sense that the aliens themselves were stalking them. The dark shadows created on the periphery of their vision by eerie, flickering light of the Hyperspatial gate they had just emerged from did nothing to allay her fears.

"It's the smell that I can't stand," Captain Lewis attempted to whisper to Jowista as they approached their host. It was far from a whisper, however. In Jowista's opinion, the purpose of a whisper was to quietly pass on information in a manner which precluded any surrounding listeners from knowing what the information was. Lewis seemed to think the purpose was to not only let the listeners in on the secret but also tell them, in no uncertain terms, that you were deliberately trying to keep a secret. Lewis gave his whispers a volume and pitch that meant they may as well have been shouts. It didn't even matter that the briefing notes on this species indicated that they had exceptionally acute hearing. Jowista was sure that the Lord General, thousands of light years away on Cybel Prime, had heard that undiplomatic comment. It certainly reverberated around the forested clearing in which they stood.

"Sir?" Jowista knew from long and bitter experience that the only safe way to deal with military faux pas was to pretend they never happened while carefully recording and filing evidence for later review at the inevitable tribunal. You certainly did not correct a senior military officer in front of another species, no matter how inferior the officer in question considered said species to be. Keeping a neutral stance was best, 'Sir' was a suitably neutral word.

"Well, they clearly don't wash, that fur looks unkempt and I am sure they roll in their own faeces. I mean, look at them..."

Jowista did indeed look at them and her first opinion was that the briefing notes had not done the 'People of Dagda' justice at all. The notes discussed physiological details, scans, examinations, even some rare dissections and went on at length about bone structure, muscle architecture, adaptation to environmental factors and speculation on evolutionary origin which the notes postulated as being canine or vulpine. There were diagrams, photographs, blurry video footage and reams of anecdotal evidence of 'the mighty warriors in action' but none of it really compared to seeing a live Dagdan warrior in the flesh. The one that stood in front of Lewis, Jowista and their entourage of soldiers was clearly a prime specimen. It towered over their party by almost a whole foot in height and it was clear that under the dark fur, which Jowista was quick to note was not unkempt but clean and rather well brushed, taut and well toned muscles were stretched like cables. The elongated muzzle that formed its mouth was filled with long, sharp teeth. The only smell that Jowista could detect was the faint hint of musky sweat with overtones of leather and woodsmoke. Her reading of the briefing notes had given her the impression that a species that had a more potent sense of smell than the average Cybel and who observed a number of societal rituals based around scent, would certainly not routinely smell of anything offensive.

"Sir," she whispered "The ritual."

36

"Oh, that awful thing." He sighed heavily. "Very well, for the good of the Empire and the glory of the Lord General." He spoke as if he were about to march alone into overwhelming enemy fire rather than perform a small act of diplomacy. He strode forward, chest firm and legs straight, one arm hanging straight down with thumbs aligned perfectly to the line of his dress uniform trousers, the other gripping the hilt of the ceremonial sword. He drew it smoothly from its scabbard and smartly snapped it into position with the naked blade a precise inch from Lewis's sharply etched nose, the black gloved hand holding the hilt on the end of an arm held firmly at a 90 degree angle.

Jowista watched concerned, hoping that the team of Xeno-anthropologists had done their job properly, as Lewis swept the blade down so that it struck the gloved palm of his other hand and shifted his grip on the hilt. The sword was now held like an offering, a gift but, and this was important from what the experts said, still held in the hand in a way which meant it could very quickly be turned into a more offensive posture. The words of Anwynn, the great shaman of Dagda, came back to her then as she had first saw them written on a vellum parchment in a Hi Def image attached to a report. *My sword is yours but only a fool holds a blade so that it can never be used.* The alien looked down at the offered blade, its brown eyes deep and searching. Then he turned to one of his entourage and grunted something in their incomprehensible language. Jowista was convinced she heard something like a grunted snicker. *They think we are silly but hopefully that is not a bad thing.* Finally, the Dagdan warrior inclined his head in grudging acceptance, *we're in,* thought Jowista. *Now we just have to complete the job.*

***

As the warrior led the group into the village, Jowista reflected on the mission briefing that had led her to this point. The primary mission was simple: Captain Lewis was to meet with the Chieftain of this tribe, discuss trade agreements and reassure him that the Cybel empire was not about to annex this planet. However, she had been given a secondary brief. She was a Gatetech, someone with knowledge of the complicated physics behind the theory and practice of Gate usage. It was a rare skill that was highly prized by the Cybel hierarchy because of the obvious benefits of the ancient, alien technology. When she had been at University, studying Xeno-anthropology in preparation for a career studying alien cultures, it had been discovered that she had an affinity with the Gates. Without even bothering to ask her thoughts on the situation, she had been immediately reassigned to a course in advanced physics and applied Gate Technology. Now she escorted diplomatic and military missions when they used the Gates to travel; ensuring a safe, timely and accurate arrival.

Someone in the military had noted that the Dagdans were remarkably good at using the Gates. Yet they did not seem to use any safety equipment or any navigation computers or any of the advanced technology that Cybel Gatetechs used. Jowista, with her two years of Xenoanthropology study and Gatetech skills, had been assigned to covertly observe and study, maybe even speak to one of the fabled Shaman of Dagda, the Priests and Wisemen who seemed to be the only ones who used the Gates.

She noticed that she could still hear the drums, even this far from the Gate where the drummers were, if anything, they seemed louder the further away they walked but she knew that made no sense. Each beat lanced into her brain, causing her to feel dizzy and nauseous, forcing her to focus on every breath and step in order to keep walking.

The village was a scene of gentle idyll. The buildings were comprised of a wooden frame with wicker walls coated with a mixture of mud and animal dung. Most of them were small huts, clearly single person dwellings, but there were some larger structures which served as public buildings. She assumed one of these was the meeting hall. In the centre, an open space served as a general communal area in which were scattered a number of cooking fires, each tended by a few Dagdans, mostly females and the young. Others were scattered around, either sitting or standing, engaged in a number of tasks that included primitive crafts, quiet discussions and, on the edge of the clearing, weapons practice.

The squad marched into this quiet, rural peace like a space wreck and Jowista felt immediately guilty. She always felt that awkward embarrassment whenever the more brutal aspects of her culture encountered others. A colonial guilt that always filled her with the urge to quietly apologise. Around them the Dagdans stopped what they were doing to glare angrily at the stomping soldiers in their heavy, black combat suits.

The drums were at their loudest here, far from the gate, repeating endlessly the same pattern of beats but varying the tone and overlaying it with more complex and changing harmonies. To Jowista it felt like the beat was insinuating itself into her mind, as if rather than beating on skins of stretched leather they were striking her nerve endings. Each beat sent a jolt of energy throughout her body, causing the hair on the back of her neck to stand on end, her skin to crawl and her eyes to throb causing her vision to distort.

"Are you alright, Doctor?" Lewis was speaking to her but his voice seemed far away and suffering from some strange Doppler effect that caused it to vibrate. She blinked and tried to focus on him.

"Sorry, Sir. I'm a little distracted. Those damn drums."

Lewis gave her a strange look as if he did not understand what she was talking about. "Drums? Humph," his voice was tetchy. "I need you focussed, Doctor. While I do the diplomacy thing with the Chief of this place, you have to collect that data on their customs that R&D need." He turned to one of the troopers. "Corporal, make sure she drinks some water and stay with her while she does what is needed. Any problems, contact me. But if I am still in with the Chief, they had better be important problems." He looked around at the rest of the squad. "The rest of you are free to remain at ease for the next few hours. Just remember I want you all alert in case there is any trouble. I wouldn't put it past them to ambush us."

With that, Lewis marched self-importantly off with their guide, towards the hall and his meeting with the Chief. Jowista watched him go before sitting down on one of the many logs that littered this clearing, which she seen the Dagdans themselves use as seats. She accepted the water canteen from the Corporal and took

41

a deep swig of the cool water. Then she leant forward, putting her head in her hands in the hope that she could block out the endless rhythm. To her dismay the beat continued.

"Are you alright, Doctor?" The Corporal was standing over her, his hand on her back. "Can I get you anything? Do you need medical assistance?"

She lifted her head and smiled up at him awkwardly, realising that she could not remember his name and her vision was too blurred to read it from the nametag on his uniform. "Can't you hear them?" A glance at his expression told her he could not. She realised there was no credit in seeming insane at this point; she had a job to do. "An analgesic would be good. I think I have a migraine coming on." She gave him a weak smile.

"You do look a little pale, I'll see what I can get from the Medbox, don't go anywhere." He wandered off before she could even tell him that she had no intention of going anywhere. At this point she doubted she could even stand, never mind walk.

"You don't want chemicals, they no good." This voice, speaking reasonably good Cybel, was the grunting growl of a Dagdan. It was higher pitched than the Warriors who had met them and seemed cracked, as though the ravages of age had wearied the throat.

Female, maybe, and definitely older. Looking up confirmed this. The Dagdan that stood over her was stooped and grey furred, supported on a gnarled and carved staff of solid looking wood. Beads and other ornaments were woven into the straggly, grey mane and a collection of odd looking amulets were hanging around the neck. Some of these looked like remnants of circuit boards and broken pieces of technology wrapped in tooled leather and decorated with feathers. Her tunic was possibly wool but it was hard to tell under the ground in dirt that coated it. When she opened her long muzzle, it was clear that several of the long, sharp teeth were missing and the remaining ones were chipped and stained.

"I am Orchil, Orchil Oonagh y Broneghall, you?" A clawed hand was held out to shake. "This is your custom, yes? I heard it was and your chief did it to our chief so must be true. We shake, right? And say names? Orchil."

"Oh, yes, sorry. Caitlin. Er, Doctor Caitlin Jowista, R&D XenoAnthropologist." She took the offered hand and shook it, the fur felt wiry and the skin on the palm leathery and tough with calluses.

"Good. Names known, friends now." Orchil's speech was rapid and disjointed. "Don't take chemicals for your problem, bad for the spirits. I have what you need. Come! Quick!" Without waiting to see if she would follow, Orchil shambled off arthritically towards one of the fires. Jowista shrugged and followed, swaying slightly as she did so. By the time she reached the fire, Orchil had already poured boiling water into a small pot of what looked like a multicoloured mixture of different types of dried leaves and flowers. She pushed the pot into Jowista's hands. It had a strong, sharp and potent smell she could not identify and was a strange green-brown colour.

"There, let it settle, let it cool then drink. Don't eat the leaves, though. Important not to eat leaves, just the liquid. Good for the senses, clears the bad humours, stops the headaches. Leaves stop headaches permanently, of course. And everything else. Not an honourable death. Well, sometimes it is, when a wound is too bad to treat. Best not to eat them, though. Just drink the liquid."

Being especially wary of the leaves, Jowista took a sip of the drink and grimaced at its bitter, smoky taste.

"Oh, want some honey in it like a baby?"

"No, no. Er, thank you for your kindness." The warm liquid was already soothing the throbbing and the tunnel vision was fading. Mindful of her mission, she decided to start with Orchil.

"So, what do you think they are talking about? My Captain and your Chieftain?"

Orchil made a noise with her teeth and tongue, a clicking sound that seemed to Jowista to indicate indifference. "Nothing important."

"Not important? Surely diplomacy like this allows us to understand one another better and prevent wars?"

"Hah!" Orchil laughed a cackling, coughing laugh. "Diplomacy. Nonsense! It's continuation of war by other means. The warriors? You have to have them because conflict is part of life, but you can't have them doing nothing all day. So, you have wars to keep them busy and when the wars are over you have diplomacy to keep them busy until it is time for the next war. It makes them happy." The old Dagdan busied herself poking at the fire with a gnarled branch, causing embers to float up into the air between them.

"But surely we want to avoid war?" Jowista was working on the principle that her companion was senile, definitely not sane anyway.

"Me, you, maybe we want to avoid war," a shrug. "But the warriors? No. They don't. Better it is controlled than not though, eh? Your chief, my chief, they'll sit in that hut and preen and prance and say the right things, spout the right lies. They'll smoke and drink and make their chests look bigger than they are and spit in the fire like they always do. Meanwhile, out here over a civilised cup of tea, we Shamans can discuss the real meat of the issue, can't we?"

Jowista was aware then of a pair of aged, rheumy eyes staring straight into her eyes and felt... something... assessing her, as though weighing her soul. *She is a Shaman, one of the secretive priests of the Dagdan religion.* Much was said in the journals about the Shaman, a lot of it speculation and hearsay.

"I think you are mistaken, I'm no Shaman. We don't have a religion like yours, the first Lord General banned all such organisations when he founded the Cybel Imperial Republic millennia ago, calling them corrupt and..." Her long and well prepared explanation, drilled into her by hours of patient lecturing from her Social Control tutors in history, faded as those evaluating eyes embarrassed her into silence.

"Shaman is nothing to do with religion, a shaman is defined by what she knows not what she believes."

Damn, she knows why I'm here, she knows what I am. She kept the smile fixed in place. One thing that all the papers on the ways of the Dagdan Shaman agreed on was that they were wily and difficult to fool. Lies melted under their gaze and they plucked truth from your tongue like an apple from a tree.

"Ok, I'll be honest with you. We want to find out how you do it."

A cackle. "They all want to know about the Gates. They come here, with their subterfuges and gifts and they ask their questions and we tell them the answer and they accuse us of lying." She shrugged. "Sometimes I wonder if your people are able to accept an answer given freely."

"Can you tell me?"

"I can and will but first, a story." Orchil settled back in her seat and looked up at the canopy of trees, letting her mind wander back along the mists of memory.

"Many, many years ago, so many that it would embarrass me if I told you, I took it on myself to wander the galaxy. I wanted to learn, to see, to do. I was barely an apprentice, only just learnt how to use the Gates, and I wanted to go out there and learn all I could.

"I travelled to all the other Dagdan worlds, talked to every Shaman I could find and they taught me a lot about the Gates and how they worked, how to travel them safely. I also learnt a lot of myths and legends and one of those was about the Althari. You hear of them?"

Jowista nodded. "I have. You don't see much of them; well we have never encountered them very much. Our records indicate that they have no planets, no colonies. They are only ever encountered wandering alone or in small groups. Pale skin, delicate features, tall with long faces?"

"That's them. Strange bunch. Off on pilgrimage for their god. It's what they do. Did you know that their god talks to them all the time?"

Jowista shook her head. She realised that Orchil's strange speech pattern had faded away a little; clearly the mad old lady was just a front.

"Well," the old Shaman continued. "He does. I reckoned that their god, whatever it was, was somehow connected to the gates. You see, I noticed that you always found them near a gate and when a gate went wrong an Althari would often turn up soon afterwards and when they left the gate began to work again."

Realisation struck Jowista. "You think they are some form of maintenance crew?"

Orchil nodded. "Yes, yes! You see, their 'god' speaks to them and tells them where gates may be broken. They travel to that gate and fix it."

Jowista thought about this, it certainly made sense to her. Clearly whatever the Althari were talking to in their minds was some form of control system, possibly a vast AI responsible for the gates. For centuries, the Cybel Gate scientists had been postulating what controlled the network. It seemed that she had picked up an important clue.

"So, I thought I'd ask one what they knew about gates as they clearly know a lot."

"And what did they say?" Jowista was gripped now, eager for more information that might advance the mission.

"He said 'Transverse waves in 5 TeV initiating gigabyte transfer of information via obverse algorithm alpha. Rebooting start up sequence, initiating particle emitters and cross checking variable linkages in multi-dimensional space'. Then there was a string of random numbers."

"What? That makes no sense!"

"I know. I wrote it down and memorised it, spent hours in meditation on the words, hoping to extract some sense from it, some great epiphany. Young me thought it was some form of profound poem or riddle, like the ones we Shaman often use to teach apprentices important lessons. But it was meaningless.

Then, one day when I had long given up finding meaning, an epiphany happened."

"And? What did it mean?"

"Nothing. To me, anyway. I realised that it clearly meant something to him but nothing to me in the same way that what I am about to tell you will mean nothing to you but is important to me. Cultural differences, we cannot think in the same terms."

Jowista nodded. "I see. So if I were to ask you for your great insights into the gates what would you tell me?"

The old Dagdan grinned at her, showing her brown and cracked teeth. For a second or two Jowista held the Shaman's gaze, staring deep into those entrancing eyes. Then she felt the headache return, throbbing in her head in that maddening rhythm, and she had to avert her gaze.

"I am going to tell you to listen to the drums."

Jowista looked at Orchil and noticed that the Shaman was tapping the branch she had been poking into the fire on the ground in a regular beat. Tap tappity tap, tap tappity tap... Every time the stick hit the ground, Jowista's vision contracted and the throbbing pain pounded into her head.

"It's you!" She stood up and backed away, pointing accusingly at Orchil. "You're doing this to me! You're using some form of... of... magic." What else could explain it? A spell, a curse, an inexplicable phenomenon. Magic!

Orchil laughed. "You really that stupid? I thought you followed the great god, Science? Sit, girl, sit and let me tell you how the trick was done. And that's a rare thing, a Shaman explaining their magic so you better listen well!"

Jowista sat down cautiously, keeping an eye on the stick.

"It's just the herbs wearing off, the effect never lasts very long, not this close to the source and not a dose as small as I gave you, which is why I always keep a pot brewing. You see, I knew how long it would take to wear off and that you'd start getting the headaches again so I started tapping about that time. The rest was your mind filling in blanks."

"But, how?" Jowista took a deep breath. She had to think about this logically. "How did you know how to match your beats with the headaches?" She accepted another cup full of the tisane and drank it down quickly, feeling the effects almost immediately.

"You not figured it out yet? Pah, young people, no critical thinking. No logic. It's a wonder you ever came a Shaman. I learnt to think afore I learnt to Gatewalk, before I ever knew what Gatewalking was. What's the first lesson they teach you?"

"Safety protocols and how to calibrate the navigation equipment." Jowista smiled wanly, knowing enough about Dagdan culture to see where this conversation was going.

Orchil nodded. "Figures." She waved a hand dismissively. "Toys and fear of death, bad combination for a Gatewalker. In the spaces between, your fears come to get you and toys will not help you then. You need your wits and your skills, honed by years of debate and riddles and puzzles. And you need an efficient memory or a good mathematical brain. Both for preference."

Jowista unclipped her Gatescanner from her belt, flipped it on and looked down at the flashing display with its moving graphs and charts. No Cybel GateTech would dare walk through a gate without one. They were an essential navigation aid – storing the unique energy frequency of every gate, allowing it to be used to identify the co-ordinates of that gate in multi-dimensional space. She peered at the readout showing the sine wave pattern of the energy frequency of the nearest gate and the germ of an idea began to form in her mind.

"I know how you do it!" She stared into Orchil's eyes as she made that statement. The old Dagdan was unmoved.

"You think you know? How can you be sure?" There was a glint in her rheumy old eyes.

"I'm... er," she paused and considered. How sure was she? How much was she willing to risk finding out?

"I'm sure."

Orchil looked at her appraisingly. "There is a test we do, when an apprentice thinks they are ready, thinks they know the secret. We never tell them the secret, though we may hint at it. When they think they know it, they come to us for the Test of the Gate." Her mouth yawed, her long tongue running over her rotted teeth. "The test is simple, walk into a Gate and emerge at the other end. But," she held up an admonishing finger, "you must walk the gate with no help, no toys, no protections. Using only the contents of your own mind, you must enter Gatespace and find your way to another gate then home again. If you pass, you are a Shaman."

"And if I fail?"

"To fail is to die. And if you are not correct in your interpretation of the secret you will certainly fail."

"I am sure." Jowista sounded certain but deep down she really hoped her interpretation was correct.

***

The walk through the woods back towards the Gate gave Jowista much time to think about what she had just agreed to do. Next to her, Orchil was shuffling along the rough path, muttering to herself. When she'd first realised what it was that Orchil had been telling her, Jowista had been sure that she'd cracked the secret of the Dagdan Gatetechs, the secret behind the drumbeats. Now, she was beginning to have doubts. *It can't be that easy, can it? Surely one of the other Cybel researchers who had come here would have come up with the same idea?* Well, it was too late now. There was no way she could back out of this challenge now, not without losing face.

The drum beats that she knew now were partly in her mind were getting stronger, more urgent as they approached the gate and that gave her some reassurance that she was correct. The beats of the real drummers matched the ones in her mind. She had to focus to stay upright despite the pain.

The gate loomed in front of them. Two tall pillars of a metal alloy no scientist had ever been able to analyse, flickering with lights. Unlike the Gates on Cybel worlds, which were usually kept clean and free of markings, these pillars were covered in mud, moss and lichen. The vivid green leaves and tendrils of a creeping plant, sprouting with white berries, were even crawling up one pillar. Here and there on the smooth, silver surface were daubed symbols in the Dagdan language. Jowista knew from her studies that they were prayers to the Spirits that dwelled in the gates. They were asking for safe passage to all that passed through.

They stopped in front of the gate and Orchil raised her hands dramatically. The gate answered her gesture and flickered into life, energies coursing and coruscating in the space between the two pillars. Jowista wondered how she did that, how she activated the gate without seeming to touch it, she suspected it was another Shaman trick. She'd learned that the Shaman were experts in flashy misdirection and prestidigitation. Orchil stepped aside and pointed to the gate.

"Now, you show us if you know the secret or not."

Jowista faced the gate and took a deep breath. Slowly and with great care, she removed her Gatescanner from her belt and laid it on the ground. She removed her boots and unzipped her jumpsuit and stepped out of it. Then, barefoot and dressed only in her military issue shorts and vest, she readied herself to enter Gatespace. Just as she was getting ready to step into the gate, she heard shouts coming from the woods.

"Doctor Jowista, you will immediately cease this activity and return yourself to your proper uniformed state!"

Captain Lewis was running through the woods, followed by the rest of the squad and a number of Dagdans, including one she assumed was the Chieftain from his build and elaborate dress. He was buttoning his uniform jacket and looked dishevelled. As Jowista turned to look at him, she could not help notice some form of food stain on the front of his jacket. As he raced across the clearing to stand in front of her, she also noted that his pupils were dilated and his eyes bloodshot. Orchil had been right about what had been going on in the Chieftain's hut.

"Doctor, you are in violation of Cybel Imperium Health and Safety regulations regarding the proper use of gate technology." In his exasperation, he was spraying spit everywhere as he came to stand in front of her. "As officer responsible for this mission, you are seconded under my authority and I must insist that you stand down immediately or face censure and court martial. Do you understand me?"

"I understand perfectly, Sir." Jowista pulled off a perfect salute. "However, my authority in this matter supersedes yours and responsibility for any repercussions rests with Commodore Artois as I am following his orders, sir."

That temporarily confused him but, like all military officers, he soon recovered. He changed tack.

"Doctor, I strongly advise you against this course of action. You are risking your life and sanity."

"I know what I am doing, sir. It's all about the drum beats. I just have to listen to them and work out what they mean."

"I am not sure I understand you, Doctor."

I'm not sure either, she thought. *But it does make sense. The beat of the drum matches the frequency of the gate energy, the Dagdan Shaman senses that beat. They can hear it in Gatespace and track it back home.*

"Just trust me, sir, please. I know I can do this."

Lewis said nothing more. He just sighed and backed away.

Jowista looked at Orchil. The ancient Dagdan turned her head to one side in an expression of query. "Are you ready?"

She nodded. "As ready as I will ever be."

She stepped forward into the oblivion of Gatespace.

***

"... and that was the last we saw of her." Lewis was sitting stiffly in his seat as he delivered his report to Commodore Artois. Artois himself sat at the other side of his desk, reviewing the written logs of the mission on his datapad. "As you can see, sir, I noted her in the logs as MIA. However, my personal belief is that no one can survive unprotected Gatewalking."

Artois grunted. "And yet the Dagdans do it all the time." He threw the datapad down onto his desk. "Do you think she found the secret, Lewis?"

Lewis shook his head. "Whatever the Furries do with the Gates they wouldn't have told her so easily. They'll have fed her the same crap they feed all the 'Techs. In this case, whatever they told her drove her to do something stupid and suicidal."

Artois sighed. "Looks like we'll have to arrange another mission, Captain. This time, find me a less credulous Gatetech."

Orchil watched as the water came to the boil then poured herself another cup. Around her, the village was bustling with the business of the day but an old Shaman like her could afford some time to relax. As she sipped the bitter tea, feeling it ease away the throbbing of the drum beats that always haunted her, she pulled Jowista's Gate scanner out of her bag and peered at it through the blur of her cataracts. *Pretty little thing* she mused. *Would make a wonderful amulet. Need to add some feathers to it, maybe a bead or two...*

A shadow fell across her. "I want you to teach me." She looked up to see Jowista standing there, still dressed in the vest and shorts. Both items of clothing were torn and scorched and Jowista herself was covered with small bruises, cuts and burns.

Orchil shrugged. "You passed the test. You a Shaman now, you know the secret of the drums. What more is there to teach you?"

Jowista smiled. "Everything. There is never a point when you stop learning."

"Maybe you are Shaman, after all." Orchil cackled and signalled that her new apprentice should sit. "Have you ever considered the significance of the notes between the beats, the notes you cannot hear?"

"That's ridiculous, it cannot be a note if you cannot hear it!"

"If it makes a sound at a frequency you cannot hear, is it still a sound?"

"If you mention trees falling down at this point, I am walking..."

And so the beat goes on.

Triptych of the Gates

Dagda

This could be the day I die. I have known that since I passed my Dadeni almost a year ago, since I was accepted into the tutelage of my Master. Since I began to learn the secrets of our order, since I was told how dangerous our work could be.

I kneel now in the sacred space, awaiting my fate. Drumbeats are shaking the dense trees around me but the only noise I hear is my heart, exploding in my breast and my head. Smoke swirls around me, filling my nostrils with sweet scents, intoxicating incense. I've been stripped naked, painted in all the places not covered by my fur with the signs that show Anwynn's favour, daubed with a mix of blood and caustic tree sap with symbols of endearment to the darker aspects of the goddess, Lysander. Symbols which say: 'Here is a poor traveller, goddess. Do not take him.' By tradition, I have not eaten since the night before, drunk nothing but water, done nothing but meditate. Though I am not sure if my Master would consider lying awake fretting about my impending death an appropriate form of meditation, nor would he see the dark humour in the situation were I to mention it to him. He can be a cold, hard bastard, my Master. I am not aware of ever seeing him smile.

They feed me something. A soft, sticky paste embedded with hard seeds and the flesh of berries. They push it into my dry mouth with a wooden spoon. It tastes bitter and tingles on my tongue. I do not know what is in this concoction, that is a secret even the Shaman do not know, one the apothecaries keep close to their chests. However the unmistakably sickly aroma of Whiteberry rises from the warm bowl. A potent toxin if the dose is too high, causing paralysis that impairs breathing. In the correct dose, it stimulates the mind. I can feel it stimulating mine. It occurs to me that trusting the skill of the apothecary to not poison me is the least of my worries this night.

A furred head, bristling with whiskers and fangs, looms suddenly out of the darkness and smoke. His features are blurred by the Whiteberry, the vivid grey of the fur on his snout leaving trails of afterimage as he moves before me in a dance. Paint and blood stain the fur of his face, feathers and beads hang from his mane. He growls and pulls out his Honourblade. The tiny, silver knife looks incongruous in his massive, clawed hands. I growl back, feeling strength and power flow through me as the Whiteberry works its magic, and pull out my own Honourblade. We kneel for a while, facing each other, our blades held up as if we are to duel, our eyes holding each other and each daring the other to strike. He raises his blade but I do not flinch. I do not fear the death brought by the blade, any more than I fear the painful sleep of the Whiteberry. I fear only the death brought by the emptiness that is the gate. He smiles then, the first I have ever seen, as I stare him in the eyes, those lambent, wise eyes, and dare him to kill me. He reverses the blade and slashes once across his own palm. I see the bright blood flow from the wound. I do the same, slashing my own palm so blood flows from it like a crimson stream, and we clasp our wounds together. Master and student, sharing blood for the very last time.

I stand then, on shaky legs as my Master backs away into the circle of Shaman that surround us. The drumming gets louder, the tempo increases. I feel the drumbeats as the heart beat of the world, this world, the one to which I am anchored. I look up to see the myriad stars in the fractured arch of the night sky above me, swirling and twisting in my vision. They all have a pulse, they all answer to the beat of the drum. All I need to do in order to get home is to listen for that beat.

I know then that this is the day that I will die. There is no escaping fate. As I step towards the gate, prepared to take that final short step into infinity, I know that this is the last time I will walk this earth. Even if I pass this trial of my skill as a Gatewalker, even if this physical form to which I am limited is not destroyed by the rampant, untamed energies of the void, still I will die. Walks with the Pack, the cub I was, will die. The untutored apprentice who was the barb of all the masters' jibes will be no more. In his place will stand Walks with the Wind – Shaman, gatewalker, wiseman of Dagda.

From around my neck I pull the leather cord upon which hangs the small leather pouch my Master gave to me when, at the tender age of 15, I passed my Dadeni trial and formally became his apprentice. I am no longer an apprentice; I no longer need the guidance of the voices from the ages. I must listen to my voice and my voice alone. I let the pouch fall to the ground, regretting only slightly the loss of the companionship its silent voice has given me over the past year. The howls of the observers tell me I am doing the right thing.

I step forward as the pure tones of the Shaman of Dagda rend the air in celebration of my death and potential rebirth. I step between the tall metal pillars that mark the boundaries of the gate, pausing only briefly to regard the intricate patterns daubed on it by Shaman centuries dead, and step into oblivion.

***

Avar

The name's Grundy, Havalack Grundy, but you can call me Gateman. All me friends do and I like to think I have a lot of friends. I'm a courier, a damned good one if I do say so meself. I move things from A to B, faster than you can blink. Whole star systems crossed with a single step. That's me, a glorified postman. But in this place, at this time, a decent courier can earn himself a lot of Tech.

'Course, I say 'faster than you can blink' but it's not really like that. It's what you call advertising. True, the actual travelling is fast. Some days you can cross the whole galaxy in an instant. Take a breath on one world, let it out on another. But before you get to the point where you actually get to step through the gate, there's a shit load of other stuff to do first. Like align the transductor coils and programme the transponder and lots of other things, mostly involving alignment or something or other starting with trans-. It's a lot of faff, to be honest, and I ain't got no idea why any of it is done, truth be told. The bloke who taught me all this stuff, old Arcturias, mentioned something about energies and vectors and some complex algebra crap that he said was vitally important to remember – to pass on to the next generation so it is never forgotten – but I've never been one for numbers. Too much other crap to remember, I told him. Maybe he should write it all down and stick it in a book and stop bothering me with it, I told him once. 'Course, that would have required him knowing how to write.

So long as I know what buttons to press, what wires to connect to what modules and what colour the energies should be to be safe I'm happy. That's how you make a profit in this business; getting the goods, messages or people through the gate safely and efficiently. No one cares about the mathematics any more. That's lost to the past.

Speaking of the past, take this job I have now. Old bloke walked out of the radioactive wilderness and into the tin shack that most of the regulars call Boo'z place. It ain't much, is Boo'z, but it's better than most of the pitiful excuses for bars we have left and I tend to call it an office, when I'm sober enough to call it anything. He was bent, this bloke, and frail, looked like a strong wind would knock 'im over, but I knew that to be a lie. You don't get to be that old on Avar without being tough, without having an edge. Survival of the fittest is the only law in the wilderness. He comes up to me quick as you please, no introductions. He says to me 'I want you to take a message for me.'

Peevo was his name, but he asked for me to call him Papa. It took him a while to get to the point, he talked on and on about how once this place used to be the centre of civilisation. A rich and wealthy planet, powerful and mighty. We had ships which travelled the cosmos, could use the gates to span light years with none of the risks a traveller faced now. Yadda yadda yadda. Turns out, he claims, it was the gates that did for us. They exploded, destroyed whole planets, wrecked many others. Wars and a dissatisfied, rebellious populace did for the rest. Our little world, once the hub of the whole galaxy, was caught in the middle of it all. Like I wanted a history lesson, I told him, and pushed him to get to the point. Even if he was buying the drinks, time was still Tech. He seemed reluctant, as if talking about it pained him greatly, but I had no time for bleeding hearts. Tell me the job and I'll tell you the price, that's my attitude. Powercells, tech or info, I'll accept them all. Anything 'cept that Cybel credit stuff. Never can be arsed with that electronic cash crap.

So finally he gets to the point. A friend of his had died, shot in this very bar by the Cybel. 'Friendly fire' they called it, bloody travesty to my mind. Call themselves more civilised than us an' all. Another of his friends had gone missing, walking out into the desert, consumed with grief. Peevo was looking for him, hoping that he was not also dead, and he wanted me to help. To be precise, he wanted me to take a package to someone he knew on the other side of the planet. When I heard the name of this contact, I knew the rep. Heard it enough times. She was a hunter, a seeker. Give her a name or a piece of clothing or a description even and she'll find them, no matter what they do to hide. Her skills cost almost as much as mine. Deal was I negotiate with what was in the package. Anything left was mine to keep plus a little extra when I got back. Looking at the contents of the package, it seemed fair so I shook the old coot's hand.

I have a routine I always follow when preparing for a gate jump. Some of it is what old Arcturias taught me, way back in the when. Mostly what he called 'essential safety procedures' like making sure the polarity of the coils was aligned with the thingamajig and all that crap. I do 'em cos I seen what happens if you don't. Then there's 'The Box', so important in Arcturias's mind that it deserves the capital letters. You have to take The Box with you, it can be a great help in telling you where you're going wrong. It can save your life and if it doesn't it will tell those who come after you where you went wrong so they don't make the same mistake. Some form of recording intelligence or sommat. Whatever it is, it's important.

One day old Arcturias forgot one minor but essential detail and ended up smeared across n to the fricking power of infinity dimensions. It was messy enough to watch and not pretty to experience through The Box so I don't have a wish to experience it first hand. So there are the extra things I do, things old Arcturias didn't and I wonder if his fate was more because he didn't do these than any 'essential safety procedures'. Take one example: I have a chip, a simple plastic gambling chip, which I have carried with me on every trip. One side is blank; the other bears the name VITSO. He's the guy who owns most of the casinos in this part of the world and many of the bars and brothels. I figure he's a lucky guy so his name must be lucky so I flip the chip. I stand there, my face shining in the reflected lights of the energies from the active gate, and I flip this chip and catch it in my hand and look at the visible face. If I see VITSO I jump, I hold my breath and leap across the unknown into infinity. If I don't see the name, I bail. Nothing on the planet would make me take the risk no matter how safe it seems, no matter how many 'procedures' are done. I simply don't jump.

So, I stand there now in the reflected light of the cosmos while the old coot watches me, and I flip the chip. It lands in my hand and I look down at the face which is showing. VITSO stares up at me. I take the final step into oblivion.

***

Cybel

"Lieutenant Icarus, Lieutenant Icarus, please report to gate 4. Gate 4, Lieutenant Icarus."

It's time for me to go to work. Barely in bed it seems, and already they are calling me for my next shift. I struggle out of my billet, being careful to return the bedding to the regulation neatness – grey blanket so flat a coin can be bounced from it; white sheet folded a regulation 15 hekatrines over the blanket. Every bed the same, done by the book. I've seen men shot for not obeying it. At least that is what I tell the rookies. Truth be told, though an officer has the right to shoot a man for any indiscretion, few have ever gone so far.

It is not long until I am dressed, turned out neatly in a freshly pressed jumpsuit with my rank insignia and commendations stitched on. I am proud of those commendations. One hundred successful jumps. No mean score. It is no wonder that some of the squads consider me a good luck charm and no surprise that many of the Captains request my services by name. I know I am good, possibly the best the Empire has, but only I know that I could be better.

The journey to work is a short one. Endless, anonymous corridors fill this place like a maze but my dorm is only a few doors away from the chamber. They like to keep us close to where we work. It's more efficient that way. I spend the journey in quiet contemplation, wondering what challenges the day ahead will bring.

I step into the gate chamber, barely acknowledging the vast dome in which we house this most technological of miracles. I head for my terminal, enter my access codes and check the day's schedule. I realise as I look at the calendar entries laid out before me that I have begun to lose track of the days. Each one the same, flowing together in my memory so that I have no recollection when particular missions are due nor when I agreed to complete certain repair jobs by. The situation in the base does not help – isolated from the sunlight and the seasons I am unaware of the passage of time. I find myself longing for the brief respite of a period of leave or at least a mission away from Cybel space.

Something, anything, to end the monotony. My only guide is the computer, replacing my fragile memory with hard facts and reminding me each day of what it is I need to do before I can seek rest. A hard and logical taskmaster.

Captain Troy's squad is the first one listed on my manifest for the day. This is good, Troy is one of the better military commanders. She is strict and uncompromising but respects competence. She's not the sort of insecure officer who would have a man shot for not leaving his bed as regulations demand but she has certainly been known to make those who do wish she had shot them. Her squad has gained a reputation for efficiency and have so far never failed a mission. Barrack's rumour suggests they are more afraid of her than they are of death.

I turn and salute as she enters the chamber, kitted out in full battledress and carrying a pulse rifle. Her squad follow her, similarly dressed and equipped, and stand to attention, awaiting orders. I salute as Troy steps forward and presents the datapad holding the transponder codes and mission orders to me. I upload them to my terminal and review the specifics. Gate co-ords 453987alpha, a small moon orbiting a gas giant in the Ceres system. A penal mining colony supplying rare ores to the glorious Cybel Empire and staffed mainly by Syntha and criminal slave labour. Somehow I expected one of my missions today to include this location; last night's newsfeeds had reported an uprising among the populace. Captain Troy's orders are to quell the uprising by any means necessary. Harsh discipline, true, but in these times of hardship a society must pull together to survive. Dissenters must be weeded from the population lest they weaken the Empire.

I make the safety checks, clicking the computerised check list as I go. A thousand things can go wrong with gate travel, the majority of them fatal. I am always careful to ensure every step is done exactly as listed in the GateTech Protocol handbook. Any variation on procedure could kill those travelling through Gatespace and, if I survived, lead to my execution for dereliction of duty. I am therefore careful not to deviate, though sometimes I wonder if the procedures cannot be improved upon in some way.

The gate churns into activity, the hairs on the back of my neck stand on end as the subsonic harmonics vibrate along my spine. I check the readouts, the going is green. I make my final log report, indicating my agreement that all is well and signal to the squad that they can proceed. They walk forward, weapons ready for a possibly hostile reception at the other end, and vanish into gate-space.

It is then that things start to go wrong. I look down at the readouts and see a red light flashing at me to abort. It is too late to abort, the travellers have already gone. I force myself to stop panicking, call upon all the years of discipline and training in the military to channel my energy into formulating a possible solution. I focus on the readings, a 0.2 phase variance in the α-energy channel is indicated. Normally this is not a problem but this time it is being amplified by something else. I scroll through the error logs and spot it, a dissonance variable in the 24th dimensional vector calculation. It was not there when I activated the gate, this is deliberate sabotage. A few more checks reveal that the sabotage is being performed by someone at the exit point of the gate. One of the dissenting miners is trying to kill the special ops squad sent to subdue them. What scares me more than this is the fact that a mere miner is a competent enough Gatetech to pull this off.

I have to think fast. I try a few countermeasures but my opponent is good, too good for a miner. I am beginning to believe that the dissenters have some expert help. I realise that I have less than a minute to safely open the exit gate before the squad are lost forever. Given longer I could do something, tap out a quick algorithm to force an exit, maybe get them out safely if not at the intended destination, but I know I do not have the time nor the skill to do this. I have two choices remaining to me now. Either I let them die and fail my primary duty or... Or I break the rules. Given the circumstances, I really have no choice.

I open up a pouch on my jumpsuit and feel the soft leather of the fetish I always keep secreted there. I don't pull it out, too many cameras, too great a risk of discovery, but I fondle it and let my mind wander. I connect with the intelligence within. Time seems to slow as my mind opens.

I found the fetish during a mission to a Dagdan planet several years ago. We'd chased a marauding band of Avar mutants through a gate and ended up in a lush woodland. By the time we'd got to the village, they had wiped them all out with the energy weapons they were carrying. Perhaps we shouldn't have stopped to try to apologise to the locals for the friendly fire incident. We had taken care of the mutants and, while clearing out the corpses of the dead villagers, I had found this small leather pouch covered in beads and decorated in intricate knotwork. For some reason, I had picked it up; it was almost as if it called to me. It was only later, after I scanned it, that I worked out what it was I had acquired. Inside the pouch was a complex, highly advanced technological device composed of crystalline structures and powerful energycells. It talked to the gates, told them what to do. Even stranger, it talked to me.

I spent many long nights in my quarters when I should be asleep, staring up at those few stars I could see through the thick blanket of noxious smog that coats our city. Feeling trapped and alone in the urban metropolis that covers all of Cybel I, trapped between stone and metal below and pollution above. We talked of many things, the device and I, but mainly about the gates and how they worked. What I learned surprised me. We had always considered the Dagdans to be primitive and bestial, with no concept of technology. However, the evidence of the device suggested that all their supposedly superstitious ritual disguised a remarkable intuitive grasp of gate mechanics. The Journal of Extra-Spatial Research logs several centuries' worth of research into the gates and how they work, thousands of volumes of papers and comments by generations of GateTechs like me. However, none of them truly understand the subtleties in the way that they so arrogantly claim. This device taught me more than any journal ever could.

I kept the device a secret. As much as it benefited my career by giving me that extra edge, it was not done for Imperial Gatetechs to be seen to be talking to themselves or relying on technology created by a primitive, uncivilised race. I had no desire to be dragged off to the tender mercies of the Social Control Psychiatric care council. I had used it sparingly, only when absolutely necessary. It gave me an edge; an extra intuitive, almost animal thought pattern that allowed me to cut through any mathematical problem with ease. It helped make me the best, but it also made me aware that I could be so much better.

As the alien device locks onto my thought patterns, I see the solution to the problem in an instant. A simple crossfade cut, slicing the gate energy pattern through the centre. By manipulating the energy flow in a random modulation, I can slice through all the blocks. This is an illegal procedure according to the handbook, the energy flashback would channel through the exit point and likely kill anyone within a short distance. However, in this instance I believe the hierarchy would consider the procedure warranted to preserve the lives of valued citizens of the Empire and the loss of any dissident miners acceptable. I have no qualms as I tap out the required command codes.

The deed done, I close down the gate, relaxing as the shut down proceeds smoothly and the subsonic hum becomes audible and finally dies. In the short time I have before the next mission squad walks in, I lean back in my chair and dream my special dream. One day, I think, I shall leave this dead world and travel to one of the Dagdan planets. There I will seek out one of their Shaman and beg him to teach me, beg him to tell me the secrets that are only hinted at by the device's nocturnal whispers.

Then, I will return to the Empire and force them to treat me and my skills seriously.

Transformations

The dance was ancient, only the music was different. She danced as she had danced for centuries, with wild abandon and erotic allure. Each throb of the music that reverberated around the club, each beat of the drum or scream of a guitar, saw her body move in ways that drew the eye. Her eyes were closed, her face serene, her upper teeth were biting gently down on her lower lip as she swayed in perfect time. Everything she did was exquisitely timed, from the way she breathed to the way the long tresses of her dark hair caressed her back. Each blink of her flawlessly shadowed lids, each time they briefly hid the sapphire shine of her eyes from view, was performed as if part of the dance. To watch her dance was to realise that every other person in the room was out of step, each one dancing the wrong dance. Though she was part of the crowd, mingled in the throng, she stood out, a flashing diamond of pale skin. She did not follow the dance, she *was* the dance - mind, body and soul working together, setting the beat and calling the tune.

Brandon, standing by the bar with an untouched drink in his hand, could not help but be entranced by her. He was not alone in that. Chris, standing next to him, was practically drooling. But that was not unusual. Chris drooled over anything even vaguely female and seemed to favour quantity over quality in his relationships. Tonight, Brandon noted, his best friend was dressed to attract. He had forsaken his normal blue denim for tight black jeans and a shiny, bulky, leather jacket. His blond hair, usually carefully combed and arranged, was slicked back. He didn't need any of that, however, for he was wearing his usual confidence. In comparison, Brandon looked scruffy and untended, though he had made an effort. His unruly hair was a wild mop, despite much gel and time with a comb, and his shabby clothes never felt as though they fit him as well as they should. Besides, the girl on the dance floor was out of his league. So far out of it that there was no chance of the merest possibility of her even knowing he existed, never mind deigning to talk to him. As he watched, the heavy rock track ended and a new one began to throb from the speakers. The girl looked around, still moving with the beat, scanning the club as if looking for something or someone in particular. She paused, suddenly, shocked out of her perfect time by something she saw on the edge of the dance floor. Her pale face went whiter yet and she stepped back into the crowd of bodies that massed in the mosh pit. Brandon tried to keep track of her in the crowd, looking for that swishing hair or those scintillating eyes or those perfect breasts among the ranks of imperfect examples that thronged around her, but he soon lost sight of her. He resigned himself to the fact that he had had the best of her he was ever likely to have – the sight of her dancing. A mortal such as he could wish no better from the goddess she was. Besides, he was no longer a free agent. He was a man with a bona-fide, genuine girlfriend and he was sure that she would not appreciate him drooling after even that most unattainable woman.

Speaking of which, he looked at his watch and frowned. "Shouldn't the girls be back from the loo by now?' he shouted across the tiny distance at Chris. "They've been ages!"

Chris shook his head. "Nah, mate. They'll be a while yet. You know women and toilets."

Brandon looked puzzled. He didn't; he really didn't know women at all. Actually, he had his doubts that Chris understood them as much as he claimed, but it was not worth pushing the point. It was too noisy for any form of coherent conversation and he was happy just watching the dance floor and enjoying his drink.

***

"Phwoar! Look at the pecs on that!" Sim stopped in her tracks, causing both Tina and Helen to bump into her back as they tried to follow her out of the bathroom.

"Will you get out of the way, you're bloc..." Tina began to protest but paused as she caught a sight of the very thing that had caused her friend to gape. Helen, less prone than both her friends to displays of what she referred to as 'leching', also found her eyes widening and following the young man as he walked past them.

He was a symphony of musculature, moving easily through the crowd like a tiger through the jungle. He was dressed in black leather trousers and a long, black leather coat but his chest was bare so that every perfectly sculpted line of his hairless body was visible. Long black hair framed a smooth, young looking face with handsome, almost feminine features. As he walked past where they stood, three gawping girls, he smiled a confident smile and turned to them. With a flourish, he bowed low, looking up at them through eyelashes that were too long and dark to belong to a man. "Ladies," he said, as he came up from his bow and continued on his way. Their eyes followed him as he vanished into the crowd.

"Now that," said Sim, "is someone who could definitely cook my eggs in the morning."

Tina nodded in ready agreement. Helen just sighed and rolled her eyes. "You two are despicable, really."

Sim arched her eyebrows, turning her pretty Asian face into a vision of scepticism. "You can talk, Miss Prissy Knickers. I think you were gawping as much as we were."

Helen blushed, knowing this was true. "That's beside the point. You have a boyfriend. And you," she pointed to Tina. "You have a sort of a commitment thing with Chris that I really do not understand at all and I have Brandon. So none of us should be ogling anyone, no matter how pretty they look." *There*, she thought, *that should settle that.*

Tina sighed theatrically and pretended to feel faint, a quivering hand on her pale forehead. Strands of fine, blond hair fell over her face. "For That, all bets are off." She giggled and resumed a more natural pose. "Besides, Chris is always saying that we 'shouldn't be exclusive'." She mimed the speech marks and mimicked a deep male voice in a mocking fashion. "He thinks it means he can play around and have me waiting for him when he gets home. Well, I'd love to show him that it works both ways. That or curse him so his manhood always fails unless I am around. Not found the right curse for that yet, though." She was smiling as she said this but there was an underlying hint of bitterness and a conviction that she could maybe do what she threatened. Clearly Chris's infamous indiscretions were taking its toll on her. Tina was obsessed with the occult and claimed to be a witch. None of her friends had ever seen any evidence of this, however.

As the girls moved off through the crowd to where they had left Brandon and Chris guarding their drinks, Helen reflected on the encounter. Unlike Sim, with her dark and exotic beauty, and Tina, with her classic blond good looks, Helen knew that she was not desirable in the traditional sense. Her hair was too frizzy to look attractive; she was too tall and slightly plump. Her colouring, dark hair and skin that reddened too quickly, was a curse she had borne all her life. She was, as some had called her, 'plain and built like a farmer's daughter'. She also had a tendency for practicality and a mind which abhorred those who were fools. Those men who were not put off by her lack of beauty were usually driven away by her brusque manner and tendency to point out flaws in everything. It was why she valued Brandon so highly. He never seemed to mind her little quirks.

She trailed after her two friends, lost in her own thoughts. She did not notice the group of large, tattooed men that barged past Sim and Tina and straight into her. She staggered back and looked the leader straight in the eye. He glowered down at her, light shining off his shaven head. His eyes were deep set, so much so that there was little but shadow to be seen. However, there was still something visible in those dark depths – a glimmer of blue light. Maybe it was just the way the brightly coloured and flashing club lights were hitting the reflective surface of his eye.

"Get out the way," he grunted at her, pushing her roughly aside and striding past with his gang close behind him.

"Excuse me!" She could not believe that she was saying anything but some instincts are too strong to resist and hers made her stand up to bullies. "That is hardly polite!"

The gang froze as if suddenly turned into statues. Slowly they turned and looked at her. Helen felt like an insect under a magnifying glass, waiting for the sun to laser her to death. The leader bore down on her, pushing his face into hers. She could smell the sweat that clung to him and see the intricate detail of the tattoo that covered all of his shaven head in elaborate dragons, but she still could not see his eyes. Something at the back of her mind screamed at her that this was not normal; she should flee before it was too late.

"What was that, bitch?"

She wanted to back down, wanted to apologise to him and send him on his way. She wanted to end this horrible encounter in a peaceful and amicable manner, without him causing harm to her or anyone she knew.

However, there was a steel core within her which held her fast. She felt her friends come to stand behind her, flanking her and offering support – both physical and moral. She reflected that, in the event of a physical fight, neither girl would be much of a match for even one of these thugs, Sim's claim to be a 'kick ass kick boxer' aside. Nevertheless, it was comforting that they were prepared to make this stand with her. She called upon all the hidden reserves of her strength and straightened her back, staring him in the eyes he did not seem to have.

"I said that it is not polite to barge past people like that. I want you to apologise for your rude manner." She hoped she had pitched her voice right, that firm and controlled manner which did not brook any refusal. The voice most people responded to at some deep subconscious level because it reminded them of angry parents or teachers.

He leered. "And what if we don't?"

"Then I will call out and those bouncers over there will deal with you."

It worked, he glanced aside and saw for himself the two bomber jacketed men she had seen out of the corner of her eye as she'd faced him down. They had spotted potential trouble and had been manoeuvring into position to deal with it.

The thug chuckled, knowing he was beaten. With mock courteousness, he bowed low. "Apologies, my dear lady, for any inconvenience we may have caused you and your companions." His apology was in no way sincere but it was more than she had hoped for. She nodded and waited for them to leave, keeping her eyes fixed on the leader.

"Come on, lads," the thug signalled his gang. "We've got work to do and can't be distracted." They headed off in the direction they were walking, towards the club exit.

Helen breathed a massive sigh of relief and collapsed into Tina's arms for a hug she felt she desperately needed. As the two girls broke off from the embrace, Helen looked up and her eye momentarily caught sight of an incredibly beautiful woman with dark hair and concerned looking, bright blue eyes. For a second, this girl looked like she was going to say something but then her eyes widened and she quickly turned and fled back into the club. Helen looked behind her and saw the gang of thugs moving back in their direction. One of them, heavily covered in tattoos of what looked like foxes, was pointing at the back of the rapidly fleeing girl as they rushed past and disappeared back into the club themselves.

Now, that is very interesting, thought Helen as she put her arms around her two friends and the three of them headed back to where they had left Brandon and Chris.

***

"There she is again!" Brandon tugged at Chris's jacket sleeve and pointed across the dance floor to where the girl was meandering her way easily through the throng. From their vantage point next to the bar, which was slightly raised above the dance floor, they had an excellent view over the whole club and Brandon could see that swaying dark hair as it moved through the crowd. Most people in that situation would tend to move like a cork, bobbing from rapid to rapid on a fast flowing stream filled with many rocks, but she moved like the stream itself. Her path simply did not seem to interact with anyone else's. It was if she knew exactly where to step in that writhing mass of people and wherever she stepped there was a space that fitted her perfectly.

Brandon watched her progress with dewy eyes. He knew he was technically betraying Helen with the thoughts he was having and that if she were to find out what he was thinking, she would be upset. However, he also knew that there was no way that he would ever have a chance with that girl and so his private erotic daydreams would have to remain forever locked in his mind. He watched her slink daintily behind one of the thick, black painted pillars that held up the roof of the club and then looked for her to emerge from the other side. She didn't. Instead the taller figure of a muscular man with long, black hair and wearing a long coat and big boots strode out from where he would have expected her to appear. He waited a bit longer before deciding that she must have walked off in another direction – away from him with the pillar still between them, blocking his view.

His reverie was broken suddenly by Chris's voice. "What the hell is happening over there?"

Brandon looked over to where his friend was pointing and saw a commotion which seemed to have been caused by a gang of skinhead thugs pushing their way through the crowd on the dance-floor. The thugs seemed to be in a hurry to get somewhere and did not care who they injured to get there.

"That's some trouble," he agreed. "Glad I am nowhere near that."

"They'll get chucked out soon enough," Chris said.

"Can't see any bouncers anywhere, surely they would be getting involved by now?"

Sure enough, the gang were happily pushing their way through the crowd without apparently notifying the bouncers that there was a problem. Where the mystery girl flowed like a stream, they cut through like a chisel through stone – creating a lot of noise and damage and with fragments of the crowd flying out from where they struck. Brandon watched them for a while, hoping that they did not get too close to where they stood. It was clear that they were heading more or less in their direction and he was about to suggest a move to safety when he heard a gentle voice.

"Excuse me, is anyone sitting there?"

He turned and almost swallowed his tongue in shock as he tried answer. It was Her! The girl he had seen on the dance floor! She was there, standing right next to him. To him! Right there! Looking at him! Talking to him! Talking to him as if he were the sort of person a girl like her would deign to speak to.

She giggled. "Are you ok? You look like you're choking?"

Chris, smooth as ever, intervened at this point. "No problem at all." He indicated the spare seat and flashed a charming smile. "Can we get you a drink?"

"Er, no, no thank you." She looked around herself nervously. "I just need to sit here for a short while, that's all."

"Well, I am sure our lives are made all the more pleasant by..." Chris's attempted cliché was cut short when the girl, with a frantic glance towards the dance floor, grabbed Brandon and dragged him off towards the back wall of the club. Chris was left, mid sentence, looking confused.

With his back up against the wall and the girl pressed up close to him, Brandon felt exposed and vulnerable. He could feel her breasts pressing into him and her hands snaking up behind his back and up his neck to his head. His nostrils filled with her scent, an alluring combination of unidentifiable floral and woody aromas. Before he could say anything, her firm lips were pressed against his in the most amazing kiss he had ever experienced.

***

"That hair..." Sim was still waxing lyrical about the gorgeous man they had seen outside the toilets. Helen sighed as she heard it, *enough already*.

"Oh, yes, the hair." Tina agreed with her friend. "The things I could do with that hair. What about his eyes, though?"

90

"Striking eyes, gorgeous eyes. Eyes you could drown in."

Helen was sick of it already. She could not deny that the man had been attractive, almost irresistibly so, but she did not think there was any need to go on and on about it. Still, they were right about those eyes. There was something about those sapphire eyes that was nagging at the back of her mind.

"Oh, no. Not them again," She heard Sim groan and looked up to see the gang of thugs emerging from the dance floor, heading towards them. Wary of another confrontation, the three girls moved quickly back against the wall to let them past. They had nothing to worry about, however, as the gang looked worried. They were all distracted by something and the dragon-tattooed leader seemed to be shouting into his mobile phone.

"Sorry, Boss, we just can't find it...." a pause while he listened. "Yes, I know it should be here but it's given us the slip..." Another pause. "What do you mean you'll have to deal with this yourself? We've got it under... Yes, I am aware of that, sir.... No, we understand... We'll sort that out now."

They marched past, heading towards the club entrance.

Relieved, the three girls pushed on through the throng to where Chris and Brandon were supposedly waiting for them to return. However, when they got there only Chris was there, alone and looking shocked. They tried to get him to tell them where Brandon was but all he could do was stare at a point near to the back of the club. Helen followed his stare and immediately wished she had not.

There, in the embrace of another woman, was her boyfriend.

Without another word she turned and stomped away, angrily pushing aside several black-clad clubbers who just happened to be in her way and trailing quiet rage behind her as she stormed off.

***

Time slipped back into its normal pace as their lips parted. Brandon gasped for breath and received a massive dose of her perfume in his nostrils. She smiled up at him prettily.

"Sorry about that." She ran her tongue over her lips. "You're a really great kisser, you know that? That girl of yours is very lucky."

"No need to apologise," Brandon managed to gasp out. "Errr... How do you know I have a girlfriend?"

"I can taste her on you." She closed her eyes in deep thought for a moment, running her tongue over her teeth as if savouring a fine wine. "She's serious, intelligent, keeps a careful eye on herself, doesn't believe how pretty she is and always worries about how others see her. That her?"

Brandon's eyes widened and he nodded. "How did..."

"You can tell these things when you have had as much experience of people as I have." She pulled away from him. "Look, I am truly sorry that I messed things up for you. You have to understand that it is a matter of life and death. My life or death, to be precise. I need to get out of here in one piece but I think they have all the exits covered..."

It took Brandon a few seconds to register what she was saying. "You need help? I can help. What sort of trouble are you in? I am sure I can help." The words came out on impulse, an automatically babbled response, but he realised that they were true. He would do anything for her, despite having only just met her.

She smiled again, "You boys are always offering to help me." She looked wistful. "But I think you're out of your depth on this one, cute though you are. Thanks for providing me with some cover, and sorry again for messing things up with your lady."

"Er, look, erm... What should I call you?"

"Probably best you don't call me, not my real name anyway. But if you must call me something, I've always liked the name Ashlin."

She backed away from him, leaving him forlorn, flashed him a final, perfect smile and was gone – wending through the crowds once again.

Brandon pushed his head back against the wall and sighed. He only had a few seconds to reflect on the meaning of the words 'messing things up with your lady' when two hard slaps, in quick succession from two different female hands belted him out of his daydreams.

"Ow! What was that for?" he whined. He opened his eyes to find himself confronted by the twin goddesses of feminine fury in the form of Sim and Tina. He knew then what the slaps were for. They glowered at him.

"Er, I can explain everything...," he said, not really sure that he could explain anything at all.

***

The girl walked confidently away from the cute boy she'd used as a shield, slinking along with her hips, swaying in time to the heavy beat of the music. She knew it was all about confidence. Whatever form you wore, wherever you wore it, you had to wear it as if you owned it. However, she knew that her luck could run out at any time. Her pursuers knew that she was here, they almost certainly had all the exits blocked and it was only a matter of time before they caught her with no means of escape. She'd avoided them so far through clever switching of forms and making the best use of crowds, and the agents that had been sent into the club were stupid enough to fall for the simplest of tricks. She knew, though, that even they could not fail to grab her eventually. She needed a plan, a means to get clean away, and she only had a limited amount of time in which to think of one.

At that point, her luck *did* run out. Ahead of her, lurking in the shadows against the wall at the edge of the dance floor, she spotted the skin-headed thugs. Who, in the same instance, also spotted her.

She looked round desperately. To her left there was wall, solid and implacable even to one of her kind; to the right, a crowd of dancers writhing to the music. In other circumstances an excellent source of cover but now nothing more than an impediment. Her only hope was to turn and run but by the time she had made that decision it was already too late. Faster than a hummingbird's wings, they were upon her and had grabbed her from behind.

She screamed.

***

"Look, you see... it's like this... this girl just, you know... came up to me and, well..." Brandon was stammering over his story, increasingly aware of how unconvinced Tina and Sim were of his innocence. It sounded like a lie even to him and he was about to try to say something more to dig himself out of the deep metaphorical hole he'd dug when a loud scream caused them all to turn. Brandon reacted immediately. "Look! See! I told you she was in trouble!" He charged off towards the sound of the disturbance. Sim, Tina and Chris followed.

He leapt on the fox tattooed back of one of the thugs, wrapping his arms around his neck and his legs around his waist, not really thinking about what he was doing - just knowing that he had to save Ashlin. For a few seconds that seemed like forever, he hung there, trying to strangle the life out of the skinhead but not really making much of an impression. The thug did not even seem aware of him. He saw Chris leap on another, this one covered in images of fierce looking bears, flailing at him with fists, only to be swiped aside with a casual sideways punch that floored him effectively. He lay gasping on the floor, clutching at his stomach.

The next thing Brandon knew, he was being spun wildly through the air and smashed into a wall with bone shattering force. He let go of his target and slid painfully to the floor. A casual kick was aimed at his stomach and left him reeling in pain. He watched through half closed eyes as Ashlin was led away from them and desperately tried to stand. He managed to get to his feet, wobbling as he did so, and pounced at the thug holding the girl. He staggered as a fist connected with his nose and there was an explosion of blood and pain. He managed to grab the thugs arm and wrench it hard, hoping to loosen his grip. He was gratified to see the girl's arm slip loose and a set of vicious looking nails claw at a surprised face. Pressing the advantage of the distraction, he aimed a foot at a groin in what he hoped was a decisive kick. The solid contact sent shockwaves of pain up his leg but, fortunately, also caused his target to fall back screaming. He was aware then of Chris coming up alongside him, wading into Fox while Eagle assailed him from the side. There was a blur of activity, fists and feet flying everywhere. Then, of a sudden, everyone stopped. Dragon, who Brandon had floored, was staggering to his feet. The reason everyone had stopped was because he was holding a knife in his hands – a massive blade, a gleaming 8 inches of steel as wide as a wrist.

He growled at Brandon and moved towards him with the knife held out in front of him. It was then, in that strange hyper- perceptive state that comes in times of stress, that Brandon noticed that there was something strange about the eyes: too deep, too dark but still with a blue light glowing from the depths. He backed away, holding his hands up in a gesture of surrender.

"You're going to regret that kick."

The knife plunged forward. Brandon tried to jump out of the way but hit a wall hard with his shoulder. He waited for the pain that told him the knife had connected. It didn't. Instead there was a swish of air and a flash of silver as the knife flew through the air and landed neatly in Sim's hand, which she had held out, waiting to catch it. Her foot was still held up, semi outstretched in a classic kickboxing position. She was poised, foot raised and ready, knife in hand, waiting to see what he would do next.

The thug sneered and turned to face her.

"My knife," he demanded, "holding out his hand. Now."

She smiled at him as her poised foot lanced out and smashed him in the face. She turned, hopping on her other foot, to face the rest of the gang – daring them to make a move. For a moment, it looked as though they were about to attack en masse but then the bouncers appeared. With some struggling and swearing from the thugs, everyone was rounded up and dragged away.

As Brandon was being manhandled by a burly, bomber-jacketed bouncer he looked around trying to spot Ashlin. There was no sign of her. Though he was disappointed not to be able to see her again, he was pleased that she seemed to have gotten away from trouble. That, as far as he was concerned, made it a successful rescue. All he had to worry about now was the fact that he was injured, possibly badly, was about to be arrested and he was more than likely a sad and lonely singleton once again.

***

The club boasted several rooms, each catering to a number of musical tastes. For those who disliked the screeching, industrial noise of the main room there were rooms for punks, 80's rockers and Goths. It was in the Goth room that Helen found herself after fleeing from the sight of Brandon kissing another woman. It seemed to fit her mood – darkly reflective, bitter, mourning lost loves. The place was also almost empty. A few were weaving on the dance floor to something slow and melodious, a long and whining intro by The Cure which Helen found difficult to place. Others were lounging around tables having in-depth discussions – leaning close to better hear what each other was saying. It was a complete contrast to the noisy, thumping menagerie out in the main room. Here the gloom reigned supreme, obscuring both the faces of the inhabitants and the shabby grime of the decor.

She bought a drink, a vodka and coke, and found a table where she could sit and be alone with her thoughts. She had no idea what to do and that, for her, was unheard of. Usually she knew exactly what the correct course of action should be in any situation – assess the problem, weigh solutions, compromise where necessary then arrive at an answer. She could do all that in seconds, usually. However, this time she was finding it difficult. He'd cheated on her, went with another woman. To her that was a mortal sin and there was only one possible ending, no excuses, no compromise. Her mother had always told her that a man who strays once will do so again therefore you never give them that second chance. Besides, she had no time for romance at her age. She had things to do. In a year or so she would be leaving university and looking for a career. Many of her friends, Tina and Sim included, believed that university was the perfect time to play around, sow wild oats and make all the stupid mistakes that you later promise yourself that you will never do again but more than likely will. However, Helen considered that a foolish philosophy. Her goal was to graduate with high honours and move into finance or politics and build a career. To do that she needed to focus and Brandon had become a distraction. There was time enough later for love.

So, the decision really wasn't all that hard...

But then, there was another voice which called to her from the depths of her subconscious. *What about the good things he does for you? The things you never noticed you needed until he was there to provide them? The attention, the affection, the silly and inane grin he did when he knew he'd done something stupid? What about the long conversations late into the night?* So, they stopped her from achieving a few things on her daily 'to do' list but at least they made her smile. And it was only a minor indiscretion, after all. But then there is no smoke without fire...

She heard the door creak open and a figure strode confidently in, long leather coat flapping behind him like the wings of a dark angel. *Oh god*, she thought, *I am thinking in clichés. What is wrong with me tonight?* Then she noticed who the person was, the handsome man who had bowed to them outside the toilet.

He stopped for a moment, just inside the doorway, and seemed to be scanning the room, looking for someone. His eyes fell on her and he glided towards her.

"Is this seat taken?" He had a beautiful voice; she would have said it was golden but again she had to suppress the urge to think in clichés. She didn't want him to sit there. She wanted to be alone. She certainly did not want some swank hunk who reckoned himself trying to chat her up. She was considering giving up men altogether. Maybe buy herself one when she was rich and trade him up for a new model every few years like a car. Maybe forget about men altogether and, if her body clock decided she wanted children later on, there were other ways to achieve that. Less messy ways. Adoption was popular.

"Please, be my guest," she found herself saying and wondered why. He grinned and collapsed into the chair, lounging like a dissolute aristocrat poet after a long night of opium and debauchery. "Thanks," he grinned across at her, flirtatiously. "I'm Ash. You know, you have the prettiest face I have seen in this place tonight."

Wow, that was brazen, she thought--and so assured. He really had no fear of rejection. Well, he'd have to get used to it now because she was going to tell him to go stuff himself.

"Oh, you are flattering me." She giggled. What was wrong with her? Was she giggling? Blushing like some Austen heroine? This was not right. *'Remember the eyes,'* that little voice in the back of her mind reminded her. Oh yes, the eyes. She took a deep breath and tried to say what she wanted to say. "Do you...." *No, focus! Don't make inane small talk. That's what he wants!* "You have..." *Idiot! Now you sound like a bumbling stuttering moron.* "I really like your...Ow!" She yelped in pain as something sharp dug into her leg. She realised that she had gripped her thigh tightly with one hand, so much so that her sharp nails were digging painfully into the flesh.

"It's you, isn't it," she managed to blurt out. "You were the girl I saw after the confrontation with those thugs. You were also the girl kissing Brandon." Because, she realised, looking at him it was all so obvious. So obvious that she could not understand how no one could have seen it before. The features were the same, especially those brilliant blue eyes. That very feminine physiognomy, that very feminine body shape, the hairless chin.

"So, what do you do? Dress up as a woman and try to seduce any idiot who can't see through the disguise? Did you do that so you could break us up and try to shag me? What sort of sick game is this?"

He laughed then, and for all that she could see through his illusions now, it was still the sound that summer would make.

"No, not a game. Unless you think of life as a game in which case my game is due to end very soon. I seduced your boy in order to force a little extra time on my part. I saw it as the best way to escape what could have been a fatal situation." He sighed. "Look, maybe this will help you understand."

As she watched, he rippled and changed. The hairless chin became even less hairy, the skin smoothing into porcelain white. The waist pinched in, the eyelashes grew, the breasts rose from deftly sculpted pectorals into soft orbs of flesh – breasts any woman would kill for, even she. The naked chest was now clothed in a tight fitted corset that allowed those breasts to be shown to their best effect.

A perfectly made up mouth curled into a smile. An unmistakably female voice spoke up. "So, who did you kill then?"

Helen looked confused. "What do you mean?"

A mischievous glint was in the sapphire eyes. "You were thinking that you would kill for these breasts," she stroked them possessively. "So who did you kill to get them? Don't you recognise them? They're yours."

Helen continued to look baffled.

"Look, it's quite simple. I saw you when I came in and thought 'I'd kill for a pair of breasts like that' but, of course, being me I don't have to kill for them. All I have to do is want it and it is mine. Of course, I do them better justice than you do. You should get them out more, put them on display. Be proud of them."

"I am not here to talk about breasts." Helen was flustered. The display of transformation had unnerved her and she was finding it hard to rationalise what she had seen. This was not merely, as she had assumed, a very feminine man playing cross dresser. What was sitting in front of her now was a woman in every sense of the word. "Who the hell are you?"

"You know the band, The Cure?" Helen nodded. "Well, I'm the bird mad girl, the girl lost in the forest all alone. I'm Placebo's Nancy Boy and Avril Lavigne's Skater Boi. I also walked in beauty like the night for Byron and was Poe's Lenore. I am all of these and more."

Certainly pretentious and arrogant, thought Helen, glowering at her in jealousy. "So, what? You thought Brandon had the potential for poetry and wanted to inspire him? Is that it? Hardly an excuse and certainly does not explain his reciprocation."

Ash said nothing in response to this. She just stood up and, as she stood, started to change. By the time she was standing over Helen, she was a he. His naked chest was level with her face, the coat hanging down and framing the well sculpted body. His scent, sweat and musk and leather, was suddenly all she could smell. She looked up and saw his eyes staring down at her from his sensitive and youthful face. He was power and strength bound up with a seductive vulnerability. She found herself having difficulty breathing.

"You know what I am; you know I am nothing more than illusion. You have a strong mind, one of the strongest I have encountered. So, resist me." He reached out and stroked her hair, then gently put his hand on the back of her head as he lowered his lips to hers. She found herself reaching her lips up to meet his, though a voice in her head screamed at her to stop – that this was foolish and stupid and he was manipulating her. Their lips touched and all practical reality dissolved. She could not help herself. In his presence all sense departed and all her mind could do was search desperately for a way to describe the experience. Lips like fire, electric contact, shivers... cliché after cliché assaulted her consciousness as she tried to rationalise the sensations and all of them falling far short of the truth. They broke apart after an eternity, and there was another cliché right there, leaving her breathless and flushed.

"There," he said gently, pushing a strand of stray hair out of her face. "Could your boy have any chance against that?"

She didn't answer him but accepted that he was telling the truth.

"I had to get away from them; they are going to kill me. I needed a convenient cover and your boy just happened to be there. Now I need a way to get out of this place alive but they have all the exits covered. I came to you to apologise for jeopardising your relationship but also because I think you have the sort of mind which may see a solution to my problem." He looked at her with pleading desperation in his eyes. "Please help me."

Helen considered the situation for a while, glaring at him...her...it? - as though weighing the price of a soul. Eventually she spoke.

"Ok, I'll help you. I'll help because those thugs are causing trouble for me and mine and also because you had the guts to come here to apologise and speak up in Brandon's defence. We need to find my friends and make some plans."

***

"What the hell have you done to this cash drawer?" The loud shout shocked Brandon from his daze. He opened his eyes and looked through them at the blurry shape of his surroundings. He was lying on a comfortable but well worn couch in a tiny and dishevelled room. Decoration was by way of ancient wallpaper, peeling off the walls in more places than it was sticking, and numerous layers of posters advertising bands and club nights. Over by a Perspex window, two figures were standing. One was tall and heavily built, the other small and slight. They seemed to be having an argument.

"I don't know. Maybe the leaves blew in from outside?" This voice was female and was confused as well as angry. "You think I put these in on purpose?"

"I don't know what to think. I got the same bullshit story from the girl behind the bar. Suddenly every cash register in this place has this crap in it and all anyone can claim is that 'they must have blew in from outside'. From where outside? We're miles from the nearest tree and, in case you hadn't checked your calendar recently, it's the middle of summer!"

"Oh, forget it." He seemed to calm down a bit. "I want a full check on the intake tonight. Someone is stiffing me somewhere and I want to know how. What the hell is he doing here?" He turned and seemed to notice Brandon for the first time.

Brandon phased out of consciousness again and missed the reply to that question. He remembered why he was there, though. The bouncers had dragged them all off. He thought they were going to be thrown out on the streets where, no doubt, the thugs would have finished them off. However, Tina and Sim had talked to the bouncers and to the girl who sat behind the cash desk in the foyer all night and explained exactly what had happened. The thugs had been thrown out and he had been allowed to rest awhile in the office with Chris. The cash desk girl had looked at them both, using a tiny and under stocked first aid box, and declared that she had no idea what she was doing but thought they may have concussion and should she call an ambulance? Then she'd left them alone because some customers had come in and then he couldn't remember anything else until now. He wondered if she'd remembered to call an ambulance and when it would arrive. It was then that Helen popped her head round the door.

"Ah, great." She sounded cheerful. Brandon could not work out if that was a good thing or not. "They told me you were in here. You coming?"

He got to his feet unsteadily. "Aren't you mad at me?"

"Whatever for?"

Ok, she was playing that game. The 'pretend it did not happen' game. He could live with that though he prevented himself from asking her if she was alright, afraid that the answer would be 'fine'. He knew what it meant when a woman said that and it was never good. Instead he asked her the question foremost in his mind, addled though it was. "Where the hell are we going?"

"To the ladies loo. We have to get you ready so you can be a hero for your dream girl."

He looked at her face. Was she smiling? Yes, there was an amused grin on her face. Ah, he thought. That cannot be good.

***

Outside, dark forces were gathering. The thugs were waiting, knives ready, for their prey to emerge. Upon being unceremoniously ejected from the club, they had rendezvoused with the rest of their gang who had been assigned the task of guarding all the exits. Now they were waiting, clutching knives in tattooed hands, pacing impatiently, their breath steaming in the air despite the warmth of the summer night.

A dark suited man was there. He did not appear, as if by magic, nor did he walk towards them or get out of a car or any of the many ways he could have arrived. He was simply there. One minute he was not there, the next he had always been there. That was the odd thing most people noticed about this man, if they noticed him at all. He had just *always* been there.

"The deviant is still inside." It was not a question, and it did not seem to be spoken by the figure, but somehow materialised out of some dark space near to where the figure was stood. "It will emerge soon. We just have to be patient." The voice was flat, toneless with a vague sense of distance as though the real speaker was not there at all but far away. Again, there was the sense of *knowing*. The thugs, had they been capable of abstract thought, may have speculated on this and considered who it was they actually served. However, they had been created purely as servitors and were not encouraged to think. They only had to follow orders, to conduct the hunt and use what animal cunning their nature allowed them to the best benefit, leaving the grand plans to their creator.

***

"No way." Brandon held up the offending article between this thumb and forefinger. "There is no bloody way I am wearing this."

"Oh, but you'll look so sexy," Tina cooed mockingly. "And it matches your pretty eyes."

Brandon shot her a look designed to kill and let the skirt fall to the floor. "Why can't Chris do this?"

Helen handed him more items of clothing, each of them had sacrificed an item or two in order to create a complete outfit, and tutted as she picked the skirt up off the toilet floor. "Because he is bigger round the waist than you and..."

"...and you have better legs." Sim smirked. Helen looked at her disapprovingly.

"It's hard enough persuading him as it is without you two 'helping'"

"Ok, what about one of you three?" Brandon was desperate now, looking for any escape. Helen sighed.

"I'm too fat, Tina's too blond, Sim's too dark. Can't we just pretend we've had this argument and that I won to save all the hassle of actually having the argument?"

Brandon looked resigned but made one more heroic but doomed rally against Helen's indomitable common sense. "What about my hair? I look nothing like her... er... him... er, whatever."

"Don't worry. We'll take care of the hair. As for the rest, I believe our new friend has a little magic she can perform."

While Brandon reluctantly changed in one of the cubicles and Sim wandered off to try to persuade a 'cute transvestite boy she knew' to let her use his wig, the others waited in the main area of the ladies toilet.

"So, who is it trying to kill you and why?" Tina asked the question everyone was thinking.

Ashlin, who was currently in the shape of a girl to fit in better with the surroundings, shifted her weight on the corner of the sink she had leant against. "A mortal sorcerer, someone who may have made a pact with dark powers. I don't know who or why but they seem intent on capturing me and killing me to drain me of my power. They've created constructs to hunt me – the stupid thugs who tried to capture me earlier. They are easy to fool but there may also be a more powerful summoning, an avatar of the sorcerer's own mind made flesh. A sort of physical astral form. That will be more difficult to get past."

Tina nodded. "I have heard of astral forms, but never ones that have a physical presence. That must take a lot of energy." Tina was fascinated by all things occult and was firmly of the opinion that she was a reincarnated witch from the Dark Ages, despite Helen's insistence that there were no such things as witches nor indeed anything called the 'Dark Ages'. She insisted on calling it 'Post-Roman Briton'. Nevertheless, Tina ignored all arguments and insisted that she had 'as yet untapped mystical power' and whatever her magical abilities, did know an awful lot about the subject. Helen looked at Tina's smug face as she told them all this. "So, all that reading the Fortean Times seems to have paid off? Who'd have thought all that sorcery and witchcraft crap was real?"

Tina seemed to miss the sarcasm. "Very real. I've seen some things that science cannot explain..."

"That science cannot explain *yet*," Helen's blunt refutation cut Tina short before she could elaborate on the things she had seen. She had to admit that Ashlin, with her ability to change form, currently had her baffled but she was certainly not going to use that as an excuse to jump on the first kneejerk conclusion and claim it was all 'magic'. "We have to focus on the main issue, how we defeat this thing, whatever it is."

Brandon came out of the cubicle, looking sheepish and awkward in a dark skirt and gothy top with a tight waspie tied around his waist. He stomped over to the mirror, groaning at his mannish appearance, and complained while Helen tried to apply make up to him. Finally, with his face covered in white powder, his lips and eyes carefully outlined and the long black wig Sim had secured covering his own unkempt hair he looked... Like a bloke wearing women's clothes.

"This is never going to work!" He moaned. "Look at me, I'm a freak."

Helen smiled as she adjusted his wig and brushed imaginary dust from his shoulder. "It only has to work for a short while and we have an extra edge to put into play." She stepped aside and Ashlin moved into his view. She put her hands on his shoulders and looked him in straight in the eyes. "The magic is not how you dress but how you *wear* it. The physical appearance is nothing without the image you project into their minds. Walk confidently. Look like you own the room, like you wear these clothes every day of your life and it is not unusual that you wear them now." She leant in close, he could smell her floral and woody scents once again. "I'll help you with that. All it takes is a kiss."

If anything, that kiss was even better than the one before and, during the course of it, something passed from her to Brandon. A little touch of magic, a little piece of fairy dust.

***

As he walked out of the toilet he was walking unsteadily and clumsily on the high heels that belonged to Tina and struggling to get used to Helen's skirt which he was certain kept trying to trip him up. Tina was walking alongside him, barefoot as she often preferred to be anyway, and Helen was on his other side wearing his trousers, which just about fitted. However, a few steps later and something clicked in his mind. A mental image of himself formed in his mind, an image of him as the girl he had seen dancing. Slowly, by degrees, his confidence built. His feet stopped stumbling over the heels but built up a regular heel-toe rhythm. His legs stopped stomping like a man, his hips started to sway and he held his head up high. No longer ashamed to be dressed as he was, he began to revel in it and the transformation was complete.

"Remember the plan," Helen whispered to him as they approached the exit. He nodded and sashayed past the bouncers and the woman behind the Plexiglas screen, pushed open the large glass doors and strode out through them. Straight into a large collection of tattooed, skin headed thugs.

It only has to work for a short time... Helen's words repeated themselves in his mind as he recalled the plan as she described it to him. Just a momentary distraction, enough to get their attention. He flashed them a seductive smile, making sure that they saw him and scented the aura of fairy dust upon him. As soon as he thought he had their full attention, it was time. Moving as fast as he could, he kicked off the impractical shoes and charged as fast as he could down the street. Taken by surprise, the thugs were unable to respond for a second or two but they were soon in hot pursuit. One of them pulled out a mobile phone as he ran.

Parts of his disguise were shed as he ran, the wig flying away in the wind and the waspie being wrenched off and flung behind him in the cause of being able to breathe. He turned into an alleyway, hoping to take a short cut to an area where he knew he could lose himself in a crowd of people leaving nightclubs all over the city. However, as he got to half way along the alley, there stood a figure in front of him. But then, he had always been there. Hadn't he?

The thugs slowed to a menacing walk as they entered the alley, knowing that there was nowhere for him to flee. The man in the dark suit smiled and stepped towards him.

"I have you now..." he began, his eyes narrowing as he grabbed Brandon's shoulder and pulled him into the light that seeped from the end of the alley.

"Who the hell are you?"

Fox spoke up. "What's up, boss?"

"What is up is that you morons have been chasing the wrong person. This is a decoy!" He shook Brandon roughly and pushed him over to the wall where he held him, firmly. He squeezed Brandon's shoulder, sending pain lancing through his body. "Tell me where it is, mortal, and I will make sure your death is clean and quick. Otherwise, I leave you to my pets."

"Sorry..." Brandon gasped. "Can't help you. Did you really think they'd be so stupid to tell the decoy? She's gone and you will never find her now." Despite the pain and his impending death, he felt somewhat pleased with himself. They'd won.

The dark suited image of the sorcerer snarled and flung Brandon away from him, into the gang of constructs. "Then you are of no use. Kill him." Dragon smiled evilly and grabbed Brandon's neck with his meaty hand. "I'll start with his balls and work up," he growled.

There was a sudden noise from the other end of the alley. It sounded like a voice shouting a word, but if it was a word it was nothing in the English language. It was guttural and coarse and caused Fox to scream in immense pain before vanishing.

"I don't think anyone will be starting anything anywhere, especially not with my man." Helen's voice was even and assured. "I've already had to tell one bitch to get her stinking hands off him and I am not averse to telling a lapdog to do the same."

Brandon had never been so pleased to see her before, not even that first morning when he had woken in her arms. She walked into the alley, followed by Tina, Sim and Chris.

"She's gone, as he says. You won't catch her now," She walked closer, ignoring the thugs who seemed uncertain what to do and heading for the physical projection. "But before she left, she gave us a piece of advice, a lesson in magic. Words have power, names especially have power and she knows your name." She looked the sorcerer's image in the eye.

"You're bluffing."

A smile. "Tina."

That noise again, that word which was not a word. Another of the thugs, Eagle this time, screamed and disappeared. Brandon now knew that it was Tina who was making the noise. She was holding one of her many occult amulets in her hand as she did so.

"Now," Helen's manner was almost pleasant and cheery, "either you can leave here immediately and give up any thought of tracking down our newest friend or...," a tilt of her head, "you can continue to argue while we pop your goons out of existence and, maybe, if we are feeling nasty, say the other name she taught us."

He hesitated. Helen pushed her advantage. "Tina."

"No," he held up his hands in surrender. "I can see where I am beaten." He signalled the thugs and they walked away from Brandon, coming to stand behind him so that they all faced Helen and her companions. "You had better be careful, though. Playing around in this world is dangerous; there are darker things abroad than us. Do not go meddling in things you cannot possibly understand."

"Just sod off out of here, creep," Chris made a rude gesture. "We can look after ourselves, thanks very much."

Then they were gone and, true to form, they had never been there.

Brandon ran up to Helen and put his arms around her, feeling her slump with exhaustion. Tina, Sim and Chris came in around them.

"I am glad that is over," she said. "I am not sure how much longer I could have kept up that poker face for."

Brandon looked amazed. "You were bluffing?"

She laughed. "Oh yes. There was no way we could have banished him, not without his name. I'd worked out that the thug constructs had their names tattooed on them – basically they were named for linguistic variants of the creatures that formed their tattoos. Once our new friend told us what the most likely language to use was, it was easy. His name, on the other hand, is a different matter."

She reached up and drew them all into a group hug.

"We did well. Ashlin will be well away by now and with the trail this cold there's no way to track her down." They broke apart and Helen put her arms round Brandon's shoulders.

"Now, let's get home and get you out of those wet things and into something more... comfortable." She wrinkled her nose. "And I think you need a bath. That perfume *stinks!*"

Afterword

So, now you have read these stories I'd be interested in knowing which you liked the most. In particular which, if any, of the ideas or worlds you would like to see expanded into a longer format. You can do this in a number of ways:

- By E-mail: dalascelles-writing@yahoo.co.uk

- On my Facebook page:
  https://www.facebook.com/DaLascelles

- On my blog:
  http://lurkingmusings.wordpress.com/

- On Twitter to @areteus

You could also let me know as part of a review on Goodreads or Amazon.

The story that gets the most positive feedback will be developed further into a novel length project sometime soon.

Author Bio

D.A Lascelles is a former clinical scientist turned teacher. He writes in his spare time and is the author of Gods of the Sea, a short story in the Pirates and Swashbucklers Anthology by Pulp Empire (http://pulpempire.com/mag/) and Transitions, a paranormal romance novella released by Mundania Press (http://www.mundania.com/).

Reports of a Blur/Oasis style rivalry between himself and R.A Smith are always hotly denied as are the almost non-existent rumours that they are one and the same person. They have on a number of occasions been seen standing next to one another at Steampunk fairs which proves both theories wrong. He is also, despite claims made by his students, neither Australian, Hungarian, John Travolta nor Chucky from Child's Play.

Also by the same author:

Transitions takes us on a journey through time. In modern day Birmingham, a group of university students become embroiled in a love story almost 2,000 years old as the ghost of Gaius Lucius, a Roman officer tries to reclaim his lost love.

What can Helen, a driven and ambitious student with high hopes for the future, do to solve this ancient riddle? And why is Brandon making late night visits to her house with tokens of love? From Mundania Press http://www.mundania.com